TOM SWIFT AND THE COSMIC ASTRONAUTS

THE NEW TOM SWIFT JR. ADVENTURES
BY VICTOR APPLETON II

*Tom's gauntleted right hand was caught
in the coupling!*

THE NEW TOM SWIFT JR. ADVENTURES

TOM SWIFT

AND THE COSMIC ASTRONAUTS

BY VICTOR APPLETON II

ILLUSTRATED BY GRAHAM KAYE

GROSSET & DUNLAP

NEW YORK

PUBLISHERS

CONTENTS

CHAPTER I

SKY PIRATES!

"WHAT'S up? A *new* space project?" Bud Barclay asked eagerly.

Tom Swift Jr. nodded. "I'm trying to invent an improved method of space travel—a way that will lick the cost problem."

The lanky young inventor was seated in his ultramodern glass-walled laboratory at Swift Enterprises. Although only eighteen years old, Tom was a veteran of many thrilling space voyages.

"Tell me more, pal!" demanded Bud. "Got any ideas that'll do the trick?" Husky, dark-haired Bud was Tom's copilot and closest friend.

"Hmm. Well, I think I have a—"

Tom broke off as the telephone rang. He picked it up. "Tom Swift Jr. speaking."

The next instant Tom's face blanched. *"What! The Sea Charger's been stolen?"*

His steel-blue eyes flashed and met Bud's in a

look of dismay. The *Sea Charger,* the Swifts' latest ocean-going experimental ship, had only recently been built and launched. Far surpassing any other scientific craft afloat, it had a fully equipped laboratory, a runway deck for planes, and a unique cable-drawn launching pad for space vehicles.

"Give me the details, Harlan!" Tom requested tersely. Harlan Ames was the chief of Swift Enterprises' security department.

"The message was just relayed a minute ago from our rocket base on Fearing Island. It said the *Sea Charger's* crew had been gassed and set adrift. Luckily, Captain Church still had his miniature pocket transmitter and was able to make radio contact."

"Did he give their position?"

"Right, skipper. Got a pencil?"

Tom copied down the figures as Ames reported the latitude and longitude.

"That's all we were able to learn," Ames added. "After that, the signal conked out."

"All right. Order the base to send all available seacopters and planes to the area for a rescue search," Tom said. "I'll take off from here as soon as possible."

He pressed the telephone cutoff button, then dialed his father, Tom Swift Sr., at their Enterprises office. The elder scientist was shocked at the news but wasted no words. "I'll meet you at the heliplane hangar at once, son!"

Tom and Bud dashed out of the laboratory and hopped into a jeep. There was no time to discuss the mystery as the boys sped across the grounds of the sprawling experimental station toward the Enterprises airfield.

Within minutes, the heliplane was fueled and ready for take-off. This revolutionary aircraft, dubbed "the whirling duck," was one of Tom's earlier inventions. It had pulse-jet rotors for vertical lift or hovering, but was also designed to fly as a transonic jet, with the rotors folded sleekly into the fuselage after the ship was air-borne.

"You have the crew's position, son?" Mr. Swift asked, as they climbed into the heliplane's cabin. The distinguished scientist, like his son, was lean in build but slightly shorter.

Tom checked the latitude and longitude figures on a chart. "About fifty miles southwest of the Windward Passage between Cuba and Haiti," he replied. "But Captain Church was probably dead reckoning from his last position."

Tom took the controls and the "duck" rose steeply into the blue. Soon they were spearing high over the Atlantic toward the Caribbean area at a speed faster than sound.

Half an hour later they were winging past the coral reefs of the Bahamas. Presently the green coastline of Cuba loomed on the horizon.

Tom decreased altitude as they approached the Windward Passage. Several other aircraft were already on the scene, though visible only as distant specks in the sky. Bud was able to identify three through binoculars as part of the search mission from Fearing Island.

"Two are Swift jets," he reported, "and that baby skimming low is the good old *Sea Hound!*"

The latter craft was one of Tom's ingenious diving seacopters—combination submarine-whirlybird—an atomic-powered ship able to fly, hover, or speed through the ocean depths.

Tom flicked on the radio. "Tom Jr. to all ships of rescue mission! Report at once any sign of the castaways!"

"Surely we can't miss the *Sea Charger's* crew if that position was anywhere near correct!" Mr. Swift muttered tensely, sweeping the sea below with binoculars.

"Davis to Tom! . . . I've spotted 'em, skipper!"

All three aboard the heliplane were electrified with hope as the voice of Slim Davis, piloting a seacopter, came over the radio.

"Give us a bearing, Slim!" Tom shot back.

"One-nine-five degrees. . . . About two minutes' flight from here should bring me directly over them!"

In the distance they could see Slim's vapor trail as his plane changed course sharply and shot off in a southerly direction.

The heliplane followed as the other jets and

seacopters swarmed to the scene. Within moments they sighted the lifeboat, wallowing oarless in the blue swells below. The *Sea Hound* descended to the water and began taking the castaways aboard.

Tom hovered the heliplane low over the seacopter and said, "Take over, Bud!"

"Roger!"

Tom dropped a nylon cable ladder from the cabin and climbed down to the *Sea Hound's* entry hatch. Mr. Swift followed.

Aboard the seacopter, Captain Church and his crewmen were already being served mugs of steaming coffee. Although unshaven and somewhat grimy, they looked none the worse for their brief ordeal.

"Thank heavens you're all safe!" Mr. Swift exclaimed. His eyes glowed with relief as they swept over the grinning, grateful mariners.

Both Tom and his father shook hands warmly with everyone. "Feel up to giving us the story?" Tom asked Captain Church, lean and young looking for his forty years.

"As much as I know," the captain replied. "It happened just before we changed watch at eight bells yesterday evening. A group of planes, without markings, zeroed in on us and dropped at least three bombs."

The bombs, he went on, had burst just above deck, sending out a cloud of steam and fumes which overpowered everyone aboard. When the captain and crew revived, they found themselves adrift in a lifeboat in broad daylight, without oars, and the *Sea Charger* nowhere in sight.

"Then you have no clue as to who these—these sky pirates might have been?" asked Mr. Swift, his brow furrowed in angry puzzlement.

"None at all, sir," Captain Church replied.

"We'd better notify Security at once!" Tom decided.

On the seacopter's radio the young inventor quickly made contact with Harlan Ames. After reporting the rescue of the *Sea Charger's* crew, Tom relayed Captain Church's story.

Ames was baffled. "Sounds fantastic," he commented. "I've already alerted the Coast Guard and the Navy," he went on. "Both merchant shipping and commercial aircraft have been given a description of the *Sea Charger* and instructed to keep a lookout, but no word yet."

"Good enough, Harlan. We'll keep in touch." Tom signed off.

After a quick conference, the Swifts decided that the rescued mariners should be flown back to Fearing for a medical checkup. Meanwhile, Tom and Bud would transfer to the *Sea Hound* and lead a systematic search for the hijacked experimental ship.

"I believe our aircraft should fan out and make a northerly, or perhaps northeasterly, sweep of Atlantic waters," Tom mused.

"Why so?" Mr Swift asked.

Tom pointed to a map spread out on the *Sea Hound's* chart desk. "Captain Church radioed his position based on a time-and-drift estimate from the spot where the attack occurred. Right?"

The captain nodded.

"But we picked him up almost a hundred miles south of there. My guess is that the pirates took him south on purpose, before setting the men adrift, to make us think they were taking the *Sea Charger* deeper into the Caribbean. Which means," Tom concluded, "that they probably headed just the other way—north or east."

"Shrewd thinking, son." Mr. Swift smiled appreciatively. "I quite agree."

A Swift cargo jet stood by, hovering on its jet lifters, to take the rescued crewmen aboard. Meanwhile, Mr. Swift relieved Bud in the heliplane and said he would fly it back to Shopton.

As soon as Bud boarded the seacopter, Tom radioed orders to the other aircraft and the hunt for the *Sea Charger* got under way. Hours went by as the searchers combed the waters north and east of the Caribbean. Occasionally a glimpse of a passing ship would bring one of the aircraft swooping down for a closer look. But in the main their search pattern lay over an empty expanse of ocean, since Tom felt the pirates would steer clear of the regular sea lanes.

Guided mostly by instinct, Tom slowly herded

the search planes back toward the north. From time to time, a jet would drop out and return to base for refueling. The seacopters, being atomic-powered, were able to fly for unlimited periods.

By evening the whole search group was back in home latitudes, having thoroughly covered the waters all the way north from the Caribbean. The planes turned toward Fearing Island rocket base.

"Hey, skipper! I think I see her!" Bud yelled suddenly. His eyes were glued to powerful binoculars, trained to the northwest.

Tom gunned the steering jets and sent the *Sea Hound* arrowing in the direction Bud had pointed out. But when they reached the area, nothing could be seen except a patch of low-lying cumulus clouds.

The search continued throughout the night and into the next day. But by late afternoon Tom was ready to give up. Discouraged, he radioed orders to abandon the search and flew to Fearing Island, which lay some miles off the Atlantic coast.

Tom phoned his family from the rocket base. Then he and Bud hopped back to Shopton in a Pigeon Special—one of the sleek little passenger planes manufactured by the Swift Construction Company.

"Better come home with me, pal," Tom said as they sauntered off the airfield. "Mother promised juicy, inch-thick steaks tonight."

"Hey, skipper! I think I see her!" Bud yelled

"Sold!" Bud agreed with a grin.

Tom took the wheel of the jeep and the boys sped off from the Swifts' airfield toward the town of Shopton.

Sandra, Tom's vivacious blond sister, who was a year younger and Bud's favorite date, greeted the boys at the door when they arrived at the Swifts' attractive home.

Mrs. Swift, slender and as pretty as her daughter, had prepared one of her usual delicious meals. As the mystery was discussed over dinner she remarked thoughtfully, "The *Sea Charger* may have been sunk."

"Sunk!" Tom was shocked by the idea. Yet, as he mulled it over, he was forced to admit that this would explain why all efforts to trace the stolen experimental ship had failed.

"Mrs. Swift," Bud asked, "do you think the *Sea Charger* was sunk accidentally or on purpose?"

Before she could answer, Tom's eyes suddenly blazed as an idea struck him. "Whichever it was, I think I know who is behind all this!"

CHAPTER II

THE INVISIBLE STRING

ALL eyes turned toward the young inventor.

"Tom, you mean you *know* who stole the *Sea Charger?*" Sandy demanded.

"I believe so," her brother replied, "a wealthy, unscrupulous Oriental named Li Ching. Actually, he's a man without a country. He was exiled by his own government when he offered to head a pirate group to steal scientific secrets."

Tom added that rebels were now trying to take over the country, and, if they succeeded, Li Ching would be welcome to return. In the meantime, he had become a menace to the world. Although his name was almost unknown to the general public, intelligence reports indicated that Li Ching was now carrying on what he called "reprisal actions" against top scientists of other countries whom he blamed for his ousting. He was also engaged in

11

sabotage work for the rebels against his own nation.

Sandy gasped as Tom described a few of Li Ching's exploits. "What a gruesome character to come up against! He sounds like a—a sort of international octopus!"

"He gets around," Tom agreed grimly.

Mr. Swift frowned. "That would certainly explain the *Sea Charger's* being sunk," he murmured thoughtfully. "An act of pure destruction! It fits in with reports of Li Ching's tactics, Tom. I think we should mention your idea to Security."

"Right, Dad. I'll do it now."

Tom excused himself from the table and phoned Harlan Ames. The security chief promised to check at once with the Central Intelligence Agency in Washington for any clues to Li Ching's latest activities.

When Tom returned to the dining room, his mother said worriedly, "Goodness, I hope you two Toms aren't becoming involved in another dangerous adventure." Outwardly brave and calm at all times, Mrs. Swift often felt pangs of fear for the safety of "her two inventors."

"Don't worry, Mother." Tom gave her a quick hug. "I doubt if Li Ching would dare show his face in the United States."

"He'd better not!" Sandy declared. Her blue eyes sparkled with mischief as she added, "But if that creepy old pirate ever does, I'd certainly like a chance to play one of his own tricks on him!"

Tom chuckled. "Okay, Sis. If I see a chance, I'll let you know."

Bud and Sandy tried to keep the conversation cheerful, but the rest of the evening was clouded by thoughts of the sinister Li Ching. Again and again, Tom's scientific work had brought him into danger from enemies bent on stealing his inventions or plotting against America's security.

In a previous adventure Tom had flown his Flying Lab to South America, where he had to fight for his life against a lawless organized group. Later expeditions had taken him not only into outer space but also to the far corners of the globe, including the South Pole, Africa, and the Yucatan jungles of Mexico. Only recently he and his associates had returned from an undersea voyage to the lost city of gold.

Several days went by but there was no report on the whereabouts of the *Sea Charger*. Tom busied himself in his laboratory, meanwhile, trying to solve the problem of developing a new and cheaper method of space travel.

"Any big brain waves yet on your project, boy genius?" Bud Barclay asked one afternoon as he strolled into the laboratory. Mr. Swift and Tom were intently poring over a clutter of scribbled diagrams and equations.

Tom looked up with a wry grin. "Not yet, but give us time, fly boy."

"How come you're so worried about the cost factor?" Bud persisted. "That hasn't stopped us yet and we've made it to the moon and almost to Venus."

"Fortunately we've had some government support for our space research," Mr. Swift explained. "But even so the cost has been staggering. And the only financial returns to our company have been the profits on Tom's solar batteries and from industrial uses for Lunite."

The solar batteries were amazing power units, charged by the energy of sunlight in Tom's space-wheel "factory," high above the earth's atmosphere. Lunite was a metal alloy with unique properties which had been brought back from the phantom satellite, Nestria.

"Besides," Tom went on, "all our space voyages so far have really been on an experimental basis. I'm looking ahead to a day when man can explore, and even colonize space on a large scale. To do that, we must first find a cheaper way to get there than by our present vehicles."

"Okay." Bud scratched his head thoughtfully. "Let's get down to brass tacks. Where do you start in tackling the problem?"

"Good question. That's just what we've been asking ourselves," Mr. Swift replied with a smile. "One factor is the cosmic rays encountered in space. Being harmful to humans, they necessitate the use of expensive antiradiation gear and Tomasite plastic shielding. And, of course, another expensive item is the training of space pilots—astronauts. But offhand," the scientist confessed ruefully, "I see no way at the moment of reducing the cost of either of those items."

"I see what you mean, sir," Bud agreed. He was thinking of the elaborate devices Tom had built for training his own space crews, such as the Zero-G chamber in which the men were exposed to the effects of weightlessness.

"The real hope," Tom said, "lies in finding a different type of space propulsion. As you know, Bud, most spaceships devised so far—I mean the self-contained kind which don't need rocket fuel—rely either on atomic power or some form of solar power. Our ship, the *Challenger,* uses solar batteries to operate its repelatron drive. Other ships that space scientists have dreamed up would need very, very large power-gathering equipment to collect the sun's energy."

"You mean like those whopping big space sails you made to collect energy for your solartron matter maker?" Bud asked.

Tom nodded, chuckling at the wry look on Bud's face as he himself recalled their troubles with these unwieldy objects. "Our 'collectors' were each four acres in size, and we needed a dozen of 'em. But anyhow, whether a ship uses atomic power or solar power, it's still a mighty expensive proposition."

"I'll bet you have a better idea already. Out with it!" Bud urged.

"Whoa! Don't put me on the spot!" Tom cringed jokingly, then turned serious. "Well, as a matter of fact, I do have a few ideas. Dad and I were just talking them over. But I'm not sure any of them will pan out. If only I could come up with a brand-new approach!"

"I'm sure you'll find a way, son." Tom Sr. gave the young inventor an encouraging pat on the back. "We both know that any major scientific breakthrough takes time. Just stick with it."

By the end of the day, however, Tom was feeling anything but hopeful. Every attack on the space-travel problem seemed to lead up a blind alley. To clear his brain, he decided to walk home from the plant.

As Tom neared the outskirts of Shopton, he saw several young boys in a field trying to fly a kite. But the boys were having trouble getting it aloft.

"Hey, there's Tom Swift! He'll help us!" cried Billy Barstow, the son of an Enterprises employee. The group of boys hailed the young inventor.

Tom chuckled and strolled out across the field to meet them. "What's the matter? Won't she go up?"

"Sure won't!" Billy complained. "And we spent

all afternoon building this kite. You're an expert, Tom. What's wrong?"

"From the way it's sagging, I'd say the tail's too long." Tom reeled in the kite and tore off part of the rag tail. In a few minutes he had the red kite soaring high in the blue, then turned it back to Billy.

"Oh, boy! How about that?" yelped Kenny Smith gleefully. "Just like magic!"

Tom grinned. "No magic about it," he explained. "Your kite was just tail-heavy. What makes a kite stay up, anyhow—ever stop to think?"

"The wind," Billy volunteered.

"What else?"

Tom's question brought puzzled looks. The boys could only shrug blankly.

"Well, for instance, what will happen if you let go of the string?" Tom persisted.

"The kite'll fly away," said Kenny.

"And probably keep going forever!" Billy added. "At least till the wind dies down."

"Drop the string and see what happens," Tom suggested.

Billy hesitated, then let go. At once the kite started falling toward the ground. Billy quickly grabbed the string again and reeled in. As soon as the cord was taut, the kite seemed to regain its "lift" from the wind.

"I get it now!" piped up Joe Spinzo, a bright-eyed eight-year-old. "We need the string pulling on the kite, too, to make it fly."

"Smart thinking, Joe!" Tom approved. "You see, there are three things that happen when a kite goes up in the air. Watch."

Tom picked up a stick and drew a diagram on the ground. "First," he pointed out, "there's the force of gravity which tries to pull the kite down. Second, the wind blows along the field and pushes the kite away from you. Third, you pull on the string into the wind, which makes the kite move upward in a curved arc. The string enables the kite to make use of the wind force so as to overcome the force of gravity."

"Gee, that's simple the way you explain it, Tom!" said Billy.

Tom grinned. "Actually, when you pull on the kite string you supply the force needed to keep the kite up—in the same way an aircraft engine supplies the force to keep the plane up. No engine, no flight—no string, no flight."

After chatting with the boys a few minutes longer, Tom asked them what they wanted to be when they grew up.

"Space pilots!" the trio chorused.

"Glad to hear that, fellows," Tom said. "It's one of the best jobs in the world."

He waved good-by and resumed his homeward stroll. He found himself wondering if the boys' dreams would ever come true.

"Not if we can't beat the cost factor in space travel!" Tom reflected ruefully. "Kite flying is sure cheaper!"

Kites! The word exploded in Tom's mind. He stopped short as an exciting idea struck him full force. Instead of regarding cosmic rays as a dangerous drawback to space flight, why not *make use of them* just as a kite makes use of the wind?

"I'll build a brand-new experimental craft on this principle," Tom thought elatedly, "and even call it a space kite!"

But first, Tom realized, he would have to develop a revolutionary device for utilizing the cosmic rays—a sort of cosmic reactor to convert the rays into a usable force. This force would move the spaceship, just as the wind moved the boys' kite aloft!

Suddenly an automobile horn blasted shrilly in his ear. Tom had been so deep in thought, he jumped. A white convertible whizzed past, then braked to a halt.

"Phyl!" Tom yelled, laughing. "What's the pitch—scaring a guy this way?"

The driver—a pretty girl with long dark hair flying in the breeze—flashed a mischievous smile at her "victim" and backed up. She was Phyllis Newton, daughter of Mr. Swift's old comrade-in-arms, "Uncle Ned" Newton, who now managed the Swift Construction Company. Tom considered her the most attractive date in Shopton.

"Daydreaming again, eh?" Phyl teased. "Better watch that, professor!"

"I didn't expect such distracting scenery." Tom grinned as he climbed in next to her.

She blushed a little and stepped on the accelerator. As they started off, a stake truck roared by, bearing the label SHOPTON TRUCK RENTAL COMPANY. Phyl followed, both vehicles going at a brisk speed.

Without warning, the truck suddenly stopped short. Phyl gasped and swung the wheel hard, but it was impossible to avoid a crash. With a shattering impact the convertible rammed into the rear of the truck!

CHAPTER III

SPACE KITE

IN SPITE of her tight grip on the steering wheel, Phyl was hurled sideways out of her seat and slammed against the dashboard. Tom's head struck the windshield. Both were knocked unconscious.

Minutes went by before Tom regained his senses. A trickle of blood from his forehead was running down into his left eye. Tom brushed it away, still somewhat dazed. Then he heard a moan beside him.

"Phyl!"

Alarm over her safety helped shock Tom back to full consciousness. Phyl was slumped against him. Her eyes were closed and there was a bruise on her right temple. Tom shook her gently and chafed her wrists.

"Phyl!" he repeated urgently. "Wake up!" As she opened her eyes, he asked, "Are you all right?"

"I—I hope so." She tried to smile. "I'm sorry, Tom."

"It wasn't your fault. That boneheaded truck driver slammed on his brakes without warning and we crashed into him!" For the first time, Tom realized that the truck was nowhere in sight. He scowled. "Apparently the guy cleared out without even offering to help us!"

Suddenly Tom had a fleeting suspicion that the accident might have been caused on purpose. But he decided not to alarm Phyl.

"No bones broken?" Tom inquired in sympathetic concern.

"G-guess not." Phyl winced and touched her shoulder gingerly. "I'll bet I'm black and blue, though! My shoulder must have whacked against the dashboard."

Before Tom could reply, her expression changed abruptly. She had just noticed the red smear on his forehead. "Tom! You're cut!" Phyl gasped, instantly forgetting her own bruises.

"Just a scratch."

But Phyl insisted upon stanching the flow of blood with her handkerchief. As Phyl concentrated on Tom's cut, a red convertible drew up, stopped with a squeal of brakes, then pulled over to the side of the road just ahead of them.

"Hey! What gives?" It was Bud Barclay, on his way from the plant to dinner at the Swifts' house.

He leaped out and came running toward them, giving a whistle of dismay when he saw that the front of Phyl's car had been smashed.

"Barclay to the rescue!" Tom quipped. "You sure turned up at the right time."

Tom and Phyl told him what had happened. Bud quickly checked Phyl's car and found it was no longer in driving condition. He then pushed it clear of the highway.

"Stay put, skipper!" Bud ordered when Tom tried to get out and help. Afterward, Bud insisted upon driving the two victims to the office of Dr. Emerson, the Swifts' family physician.

Dr. Emerson examined them and bandaged Tom's cut. "You're both all right, so far as I can tell," he announced. "No sign of any concussion. However, you should rest quietly—at least through tomorrow. That means in bed, young man!" the medic warned with a humorous shake of his finger at Tom.

The young inventor groaned, thinking of the loss of time from work. But he promised to comply.

Bud took Phyl home and called a towing service to get her car. Then he drove Tom to his house.

Mrs. Swift and Sandy paled at sight of Tom's bandaged forehead. After hearing what had happened, they immediately ordered him to bed. Bud walked upstairs with his pal.

"Good grief, you'd think I was facing major surgery!" Tom muttered as he changed into pajamas.

"Quiet, please! No griping allowed," Bud retorted with a chuckle, "or I'll call in a surgeon to remove that bump of stubbornness."

Then Bud became serious. "Tom, did you notice the license number of the truck?"

"No, but I saw the sign on the side. It belongs to the Shopton Truck Rental Company." Tom shot a questioning look at Bud. "Why?"

"Skipper, has it occurred to you that the crash might not have been an accident?"

Tom nodded thoughtfully. "Frankly, yes, Bud. But I didn't want to say anything in front of Phyl."

"Well, I intend to check up and find out," Bud declared. "That driver might even have run you down, if Phyl hadn't happened to pick you up!"

Tom agreed this was possible. "See what you can dig up, Bud."

The following morning, on his way to Enterprises, Bud stopped at the office of the Shopton Truck Rental Company. He explained about the crash and asked for the names and addresses of all persons who had rented trucks from the company the day before.

The manager was only too happy to oblige. Four persons had rented trucks, none of which had yet been returned. Two of the people had left town the morning before on long-distance hauling jobs.

The third proved to be a construction man who said he had been at the site of a project during the time of Phyl's accident. After inspecting the rear end of his truck, Bud was satisfied that this was not the one which had been involved in the crash.

"That leaves one name," Bud said.

But when he checked the renter, Gus Emden, he was told at the address given that no one there had ever heard of such a person. Baffled, Bud drove to the plant and reported this to Harlan Ames.

"Looks as though Emden's our boy," Ames agreed. "I'll alert the police and see if they can find him and the truck. But he probably used a phony name if he intended to cause an accident."

The second day after the accident, Dr. Emerson made an early visit at the Swift home and pronounced Tom fit to return to work. As Tom drove to Enterprises with his father, the young inventor explained his space-kite idea.

"A spaceship propelled by cosmic radiation?" Mr. Swift was at once startled and intrigued. "And yet, why not? Tom, I believe you have a really promising idea there."

Then the scientist frowned. "The only trouble is you'd need still another source of energy—something to provide a force for the cosmic radiation to react against. In other words, something to take the place of the kite string on an ordinary air kite.

Without such a device, your craft would drift out of control."

"That's true, Dad," Tom replied, "but I believe I have the answer."

"You usually do." Mr. Swift grinned proudly at his son. "Let's hear it."

"Briefly, my space kite will need a gravity concentrator," Tom went on. "Sort of a repelatron in reverse."

The repelatron was a major invention of Tom's used in his famous spaceship, the *Challenger,* in which he had reached the moon.

"My gravity concentrator will make use of the *attracting* force between objects, rather than the repelling force," Tom added.

Whirling through Tom's mind was the fact that every object in the universe attracts every other object. The earth exerts a pull to keep objects on it. The moon and the earth attract each other as do the sun and the planets.

Tom continued, "I hope to invent a device for *increasing* the gravitational pull which is exerted by the earth or any other heavenly body on my space kite. By aiming the device in the right direction—say at the earth or moon or sun or any suitable planet—the pilot will be able to produce a strong pull to act as a 'kite string' for his craft."

"Hmm. Most ingenious." Mr. Swift frowned. "But it certainly won't be easy to devise such a gravity concentrator. Also, to be effective, the device would have to step up the gravitational attraction to a strength thousands or millions of times as great as normal."

"Yes," Tom admitted, "but I think I've figured out how to tackle the problem. I'm calling my new device the gravitex."

"I wish you luck," Mr. Swift said.

Once at Swift Enterprises, Tom parted from his father and hurried to his laboratory. Quickly he sketched a design for his space kite. Then he phoned Arv Hanson, the expert who turned out scale models of the Swifts' inventions as the first step past the idea stage.

Two minutes later, Arv, a good-natured hulking six-footer, reported to the laboratory. "What's up, skipper?" he asked eagerly.

"Take a look."

Tom showed him the rough drawings of the space kite. Hanson was fired with enthusiasm.

"Boy, this makes space travel look like fun!" he exclaimed. "How soon do you want the model?"

"By yesterday." Tom grinned. "But don't break your neck, Arv. We'll work on this together."

The design of the space kite was beautifully simple. The pilot and copilot, with their control board, would be enclosed in the front part by a plain transparent plastic dome. Behind their seats, the dome was partitioned off by the flat "screen layers" of Tom's cosmic reactor—the device for converting cosmic radiation into motive power.

From the center of the reactor, a cone protruded out behind like a stubby comet's tail. This was to be the directional-aiming cone of the gravitex.

"I'll get to work on this at once," Arv promised.

He began machining the metal parts from light-weight magnesium alloy. Tom, meanwhile, shaped the glittering nose dome out of transparent plastic on a molding press. Within hours, the finished model of the space kite was hanging from the ceiling of the laboratory. It had three slender, graceful landing supports.

"Prettiest thing I've worked on in months," Arv declared as he paused to admire the result.

At that moment the outer door of the laboratory swung open. A food cart was rolled in by Chow Winkler, a plump, former-chuck-wagon cook. He

was now chef on all Enterprises expeditions, and served meals to the Swifts whenever they were working in the laboratory.

"Soup's on, buckaroos!" he boomed cheerfully. The Texan wore a green-and-red shirt, cowboy boots, and a white ten-gallon hat. It was pulled so low over his eyes that it prevented him from seeing the suspended space-kite model.

"Hey, watch it, Chow!" Tom yelled.

An instant later there was a loud *whang* as Chow collided head-on with the space kite!

The glittering model crashed to the floor, as Chow fell flat on his back. "Brand my coyote cutlets, what sneakin' varmint hit me?"

Tom and Arv helped Chow to his feet. Then Tom grinned. "Old-timer, you just sabotaged my latest invention!"

Chow stared around dazedly. "I'm sure sorry, Tom. Looks like I knocked it all galley-west. Didn't do my brand-new sombrero any good, either."

Luckily the kite model was undamaged and Tom hung it up again. Chow straightened out his tall white hat, then brushed it off. "What's this new contraption o' yours, Tom?"

"A space kite for cosmic astronauts."

Chow's leathery face assumed a puzzled expression. "What kind o' nuts did you say?"

"Not nuts—*astronauts*." Tom tried hard to suppress a smile because he did not want to embarrass the kindhearted old Westerner. "Voyagers to the stars!"

"Humph." Chow stared hard at the kite model for a few moments, then gave up trying to understand it. "Wal, it made me *see* stars, all right, but I dunno if I'd care to go ridin' up yonder in such a flimsy rig."

After lunch Arv went off to supervise the building of a full-sized pilot model of the space kite. Tom hopped on a motor scooter and headed for the security department.

"Any clues yet on the *Sea Charger,* Harlan?" he asked the security chief.

Ames shook his head. "Not yet. But it's pretty certain that the truck crash was no accident."

Ames said that the vehicle had been found by the State Police abandoned on the highway.

"We got a description of the person who rented that particular truck, but I doubt if it'll do us much good. Sounds as though he wore a disguise, including a wig."

Tom's jaw clenched at the news. It was clear that some deadly enemy was at work against the Swifts. Before he could ask any questions, the telephone rang. Harlan Ames picked it up.

"Security. Ames speaking." A moment later his face became tense. After listening a while, he snapped, "Hold it!" and turned to Tom.

"Get this, skipper. Fearing Island just received a radio call from the SS *Dragon Queen,* out of

Hong Kong for Liverpool. The ship's operator was answering our broadcasts asking for information about the *Sea Charger*. Says he picked up a strange signal several days ago—a Chinese voice speaking in Cantonese dialect. The voice said: 'Meet at midnight for fast capture!' "

Tom's eyes flashed with excitement. "Harlan, that word 'fast' may mean 'Swift.' And 'fast capture' could have referred to the *Sea Charger*."

"Yes." Ames leaned forward. "And also, Tom, it could mean you personally are in danger!"

CHAPTER IV

THE MYSTERIOUS ICEBERG

TOM'S deep-set eyes stared ahead. His jaw set resolutely as he said, "I'm prepared for danger, whatever it is. Harlan, that message in Cantonese is our best lead yet!"

"You mean it *could* tie in with Li Ching?" Ames asked.

Tom nodded. He took the phone and asked George Dilling, the communications chief at Fearing, to connect him directly to the radio receiving-and-transmitting apparatus.

"All set. Go ahead," Dilling reported a moment later.

Tom identified himself to the *Dragon Queen's* radio operator and asked for any possible information on the source of the strange signal.

"I cannot say precisely, sir," the Oriental operator replied, selecting his words carefully. "However, we did pick up the same signal twice again the next day, although not clearly enough to make out any words. Each time I attempted to take a radio bearing."

The operator then gave Tom the position obtained from his rough fix and added, "It is my belief, taking into consideration the elapsed time between signals, that the ship must be proceeding on a course approximately north-northwest. But of course that is only a guess."

"It's good enough! Many thanks for your help," Tom said. "Please keep us informed if you pick up anything more."

"Will be pleased to co-operate, sir," the Oriental radioman replied, then signed off.

Tom turned to the huge wall map on which the security department kept track of the movements of all Swift personnel, as well as their aircraft and seacraft, all over the world. He plotted the position reported by the *Dragon Queen's* operator. Then, after some quick calculations, Tom extended a great-circle course heading north-northwestward from the fix.

"What do you make of it, skipper?" Ames asked.

Tom frowned uncertainly. "If that information from the *Dragon Queen's* operator is right, the suspects are heading for the Grand Bank off Newfoundland."

Tom studied the chart closely for a few moments. Suddenly his eyes narrowed as he noticed a speck on the map which he had previously over-looked.

After consulting the navigation charts for that area, Tom exclaimed, "Harlan, I have a hunch! Before they reach the Grand Bank, they'll be passing near a small formation of rocks hardly big enough to be called an island." Tom pointed out the formation on the map. "According to the navigation charts, it's usually shrouded in fog—and would make an ideal hide-out for pirates."

"Good guess, Tom!" Ames agreed enthusiastically. "I think we should follow it up!"

"I'll handle this myself," Tom decided.

He picked up the telephone and called Bud Barclay. After explaining the mission he had in mind, Tom asked his copilot to ready a small amphibian plane.

Tom had designed the plane especially for secret flights. It had a coating of Tomasite plastic, which acted as a radiation shield, and an electromagnetic neutralizer. The plane's engines were also equipped with a special silencer device to avoid being detected.

"Roger!" Bud responded. "How soon do you want to take off?"

"This afternoon, and pronto."

Next, Tom called Felix Wong, a young Chinese-American engineer employed by Swift Enterprises. "Felix, how'd you like to take a quick jaunt up toward Newfoundland?" Tom asked. "I'm going on a secret mission. If it pays off, I may need a Chinese interpreter."

"Sounds most exciting," Felix replied with a chuckle. "I shall consider myself lucky to be included!"

"Good!" Tom briefed the good-looking, slender young Chinese on the purpose of the flight.

Shortly before four o'clock that afternoon, the three friends rendezvoused on the Enterprises airfield and climbed aboard the amphibian. On signal from the tower, Tom taxied down the airstrip. They were soon air-borne and heading out over the North Atlantic.

Strong headwinds slowed their flight, with the result that darkness had fallen long before they reached the tiny rock formation near the Grand Bank.

"Boy, that hunk of rock is just a speck on the map," Bud muttered. "This is going to be like looking for a needle in a haystack."

"*Now* they tell me!" Felix Wong groaned, but his eyes twinkled merrily in his round face. Felix was liked by everyone at the plant for his never-failing good nature.

"Don't worry." Tom winked at Felix. "Bud's my navigator on this flight, so it's his problem. If he lands us in the drink, we'll sue him!"

"A consoling thought," Felix retorted with a chuckle.

Tom checked Bud's calculations, and, as they neared the location of the small rocky island, he turned off the plane's lights. The night was overcast, with the sea visible only as a dim heaving mass below them.

Suddenly a light flickered into view near the horizon, then another. As Tom swooped lower, several more could be seen. The lights were clustered together, but revealed no clear formation.

"We've found something," Bud murmured. "But what is it—a single ship or a bunch of small boats?"

Tom checked his radarscope. To his surprise, he could pick up nothing on the screen.

"Looks as though we'll have to go down and find out in person," he said in a puzzled voice.

Tom nosed the amphibian into a steep but careful descent toward the surface of the water. Luckily the wind had abated and the waves were not high. As soon as the ship was water-borne, Tom began taxiing in the direction of the lights. Moments later, the lights suddenly vanished.

"Hey! What gives?" Bud cried out in alarm.

It was an unpleasant sensation, moving through the inky darkness with no longer even a pinpoint of light as a guide. Overhead, too, all was dark except for a faint moonglow glimmering through the clouds in one part of the sky.

Again Tom probed the darkness with the plane's radar. At first the sweep detected nothing.

But presently the scope revealed a huge object dead ahead.

"Might be an iceberg!" Bud exclaimed.

Throwing caution to the winds, Tom switched on the amphibian's powerful searchlights. Sure enough, in the blazing glare, a massive glittering iceberg lay jutting up from the water directly in their course! Within seconds, they would have crashed into it.

Tom gunned the engines and hauled back on the stick. The amphibian soared aloft, barely clearing the huge berg.

"Good night! What a close squeak!" Tom mopped the cold beads of perspiration that had burst out on his forehead.

Even Felix Wong's voice sounded strained as he murmured, "For a moment I feared we were about to meet our honorable ancestors sooner than expected!"

"What I don't understand is why the radarscope didn't pick the doggone thing up sooner," Bud complained.

"Let's just be thankful we *did* spot it in time," Tom said.

He flew over the area a while longer, continuing to check their navigational position. But they caught no further glimpse of the mysterious lights, and the radar revealed no object other than the iceberg and the rocky islet itself as indicated on the map.

At last Tom gave up the search and they flew back to Enterprises, thoroughly discouraged.

By the time he arrived home, it was past midnight. Sandy and Mrs. Swift had retired, but Mr. Swift was still up and listened to his son's story with keen interest. At its conclusion, the older scientist remarked, "It's certainly odd, Tom. But, at any rate, we should report that iceberg at once. It's a potential menace to shipping."

Mr. Swift immediately called the nearest Coast Guard station. The operator on duty promised to alert the International Iceberg Patrol by radio.

The next morning a further surprise was in store for the Swifts. Soon after Tom and his father reached their office at Enterprises, Miss Trent, their efficient secretary, switched through a call from the Coast Guard.

Mr. Swift answered. As he listened he frowned in puzzlement. "I see," he murmured with a frown. "Thank you."

"Anything wrong, Dad?" Tom asked as his father put down the instrument.

"The Iceberg Patrol reports that there are no bergs in that vicinity."

Tom's eyes widened in astonishment. "But we saw it! All of us on our plane can't be goofy!"

Mr. Swift was equally baffled. "I can't understand it either, son. But the Coast Guard assured me that the patrol checked thoroughly."

Tom had to admit the mystery had him

stumped, for the moment at least. In the meantime, he decided to resume work on the gravitex for his space kite, and on a motor scooter hurried to his laboratory.

As he assembled the materials on his workbench, the young inventor smiled. "Guess I'll have to play this by ear," he thought. "I'm trying to do something I can't even fully explain to myself!"

Tom reflected that gravity can be considered as a form of radiation even though its nature is not yet clearly understood by scientists.

"But I'm sure that my device will be able to concentrate the strength of radiation by electromagnetic action," he said to himself.

First, Tom shaped the direction cone of his gravitex on a metal-spinning lathe. Next, he molded a number of lightweight plastic balls and removed the air inside them with a vacuum pump. He then wound the balls with many turns of fine, insulated silver wire, just as if he were winding up balls of knitting wool.

"Guess I'll call these gravitol spheres," Tom decided, jotting down this name on his working sketch.

The spheres were mounted around the neck of the direction cone, then connected by cable to the electronic component through a power control unit. When power was turned on, the electricity would flow through the fine silver wires and create rapidly rotating magnetic flux inside the gravitol spheres.

Other circuits had to be wired and adjustments made. When the setup was finished, Tom bolted his gravitex to a platform, the cone pointing upward. Above this, he attached a weight to a spring balance which had a dial to indicate the force of gravity.

"So far, so good," Tom thought. "Now to see if my idea works!"

He switched on power and adjusted the voltage reading of the control unit. Instantly the needle of the gravity dial swung downward.

Tom gave a cry of delight. "It's working!"

The gravitex was concentrating and magnifying the gravitational force acting on the suspended weight.

"I want Dad to see this!" Tom muttered triumphantly. He turned a knob on the control unit, stepping up the voltage. The gravity needle responded by swinging still farther around the dial.

At the same time, Tom became aware of a strange sensation in his head. He felt giddy. "What's the matter with me?" he wondered.

The young inventor had a weird feeling of going up and up in space. He grabbed the workbench for support. His eyes would not focus right.

A second later Tom blacked out completely!

CHAPTER V

DESTINATION OUTPOST

"HEY, TOM! Where are you?"

Bud Barclay had just poked his head into the laboratory. Getting no answer to his shout, he strode forward to see what was making a hum. Bud gasped when he saw Tom sprawled unconscious on the floor beside his workbench.

"Good night! What happened to him?" With a pang of fear, Bud ran toward the young inventor, flicking off the power switch as he passed it. He raised Tom's head and felt his pulse, then grabbed the phone to summon Dr. Simpson.

"Doc, get to Tom's lab on the double!" Bud cried.

The Enterprises plant physician arrived within moments and Tom was carried to a cot in an adjoining room. To Bud's immense relief, there was no sign of injury. After a few whiffs of spirits of ammonia, Tom quickly recovered consciousness.

"Hey! You had us scared, pal!" Bud said. "What were you doing? And what's that rig on your workbench?"

Tom stared blankly for a moment, then grinned as memory returned. "Oh, you mean my new gravitex machine." Briefly, he explained its function. "I guess my invention knocked me out."

"How?"

"The gravity concentrator apparently acted as a convex magnifying lens does when you focus a beam of sunlight with it."

"I don't understand," Doc Simpson put in.

"Well, have you ever noticed how the lens creates a ring of shadow around the focused spot of light?" When Doc nodded, Tom went on, "The gravity concentrator did the same thing—that is, it created a gravity shadow around the test stand. I was working within that shadow, which meant that my gravity, or earth weight, was lessened, as it would be if I had been floating in outer space. It made me so giddy that I blacked out."

Bud scratched his head, then chuckled. "It's still a puzzle to me, but I guess it's a good thing I turned off that switch. Otherwise, I'd have gone slightly feather-headed myself!"

"You sure would have," Tom agreed. "Thanks to both of you for rescuing me!" With a happy grin the young inventor bounded to his feet. "One good thing—at least my gravitex works! All I have to do now is fix the test setup, so I won't conk out again next time I try it."

"Either that or I'd better leave you some iron pills to weigh you down," the young medic quipped. He left then to return to his duties at the Enterprises infirmary.

At noon Chow Winkler brought the two boys a lunch of hot chicken sandwiches and cherry pie. The old Westerner was curious about the invention.

"Brand my cactus salad, what's that contraption?" he asked. "Looks like a fancy brooder for raisin' biddies!"

Tom could not suppress a smile. "Actually it's a—well, a sort of weight-reducing machine."

"Hot ziggety!" the hefty chef exclaimed. "How about me usin' it first, boss?"

Tom told him the truth before the joke went any further. The cook went off with his lunch cart, mystified but impressed.

As the boys finished their dessert, Bud asked, "Will your gravitex be hard to fix? I mean, so the same trouble won't happen again."

"No. I can either mount it higher on the test stand, so I won't be inside the reduced-gravity shadow when I operate it—or I can just hook up a remote control. Guess that'll be simpler."

After the remote-control lead had been installed, Tom tried the gravitex again. Bud was astounded when he saw how much the pull was increased on the suspended weight.

"This is the 'string' for my space kite," Tom explained. "Of course with the amplifying circuits in the gravitex controls, I'll be able to step up the gravitational attraction on the craft many thousands of times."

"I still haven't seen this space kite of yours," Bud reminded the young inventor.

"Hey, that's right," Tom said. "I'll take you over and show you the model. But first I'll phone Felix Wong to come here and see this."

He demonstrated the gravitex to the young Chinese-American engineer, then asked him to build a full-scale replica for installation in the space kite. "Will do, skipper," Felix promised.

Then Tom and Bud drove by jeep to Arv Hanson's workshop which was located in another building of the experimental station. The room hummed with the noise of lathes and other machine tools. Blue-white arcs flashed from electric welders as mechanics assembled the parts of the space kite which were already complete.

"How's she coming, Arv?" Tom inquired.

"Swell. We should have it ready within forty-eight hours, barring any hitches."

Bud whistled when he saw the small gleaming model of the space kite. "Boy, she's a beauty, skipper! In a neat little sports rig like this, we can really go joy riding in space!"

There was a hopeful glint in Bud's eye as he added, "That's if you're not thinking of leaving me behind when you try 'er out."

Tom chuckled and threw an arm around his pal's shoulders. "Not if you're game to come along, Bud. I'd sure feel lost without my daredevil co-pilot!"

The boys hopped into their jeep and sped back to Tom's private laboratory. There Tom explained about the cosmic reactor which would provide the space kite with motive power.

"I plan to build one up at the space station, where I'll be able to test it out with actual radiation. Want to come along?"

Bud clicked his heels and snapped a comic salute. "How soon do we take off, sir?"

"First thing in the morning," Tom replied with a grin. "So hit the sack early."

At dawn the next day the two boys flew to Fearing Island. The Swifts' rocket base, once a bleak stretch of sand dunes and scrubgrass, was now a scene of neatly laid out barracks, workshops, and gantries. Space vehicles and future satellites bristled from the launching pads.

Tom radioed for clearance and landed on the island's airfield. The boys sped by car to the launching area where mechanics were checking and fueling one of the cargo rockets.

"Take-off within an hour," a technician reported.

Fifty minutes later Tom, Bud, and their crew lay strapped to acceleration couches inside the spaceship's flight compartment. Loud-speakers blared out the countdown.

Then came the thunderous roar of blast-off. Smoke and flame billowed from the launching pad, and an instant later the gleaming rocket zoomed upward toward the ionosphere.

A red light flashed on the control panel as the first stage of the rocket motor was jettisoned by the automatic release gun. Minutes later, the second stage was cut loose, its noisy explosion followed by an awesome silence.

"Smooth trip," Bud observed.

As the G pressure eased, the crew swung their couches upright and unstrapped their safety belts. They were now coasting upward into orbit.

"Let's take a look at little old earth," Tom said jokingly. He pressed a button and the inside canopy of the flight cabin slid back. All about the special glass dome was an inky void, dotted with the steely glitter of distant stars. Below, the earth was revealed as a globe floating in the darkness.

"Guess I'll never get over the feeling that magnificent sight gives me," Bud muttered.

For the next four hours the astronauts coasted through space at a velocity of thousands of miles per hour. Then, as the cosmic-ray altimeter flashed its red warning signal, Tom fired the steering motors to tilt the ship into orbital flight.

As the punched flight tape unreeled through the Spacelane Brain, Tom watched the radar screen. It should be picking up the Swifts' outpost. Tom was puzzled. The radar showed absolutely no sign of the gleaming silver sky wheel!

Bob Jeffers, a young crewman, flashed Tom a perplexed look. "What gives, skipper?"

"I'd like to know too," Bud blurted out anxiously. "Do you think the space station went off course?"

"Not likely, without help, Bud."

"Then you mean those unknown enemies of yours, headed by Li Ching, are operating in space, and could have stolen it?" Bud exclaimed.

"They probably are working in space," Tom replied thoughtfully. "But I doubt that they've stolen the outpost. I admit something's wrong—but I think maybe our navigation system's in error."

Bud's eyes met Tom's. "Sabotage?" he murmured.

"Maybe. I'd better find out right now."

Tom pulled a kit from a locker, selected some instruments, then quickly checked the Spacelane Brain. This device combined both the navigational instruments and the automatic pilot into a single navigating-steering mechanism.

"Any sign of a foul-up?" Bud asked as Tom finished his check.

Again Tom shook his head. "Everything seems okay. I can't understand it, Bud."

The young inventor was silent for several seconds. Then he ordered those aboard to assist in a fast trouble-shooting trace-through of the servo-system controls by which the Brain's commands were transmitted to the steering motors. This check too revealed nothing wrong.

"There's only one answer I can think of," Tom told the others. "Li Ching or his buddies must be getting through our Tomasite shielding. They're using some sort of electromagnetic-wave action which affects our control system."

The crewmen stared at Tom uneasily. "What can we do, skipper?" one asked.

"First I'll go outside and check our position," Tom replied. "While I'm at it, I'll see if our space-suit mechanisms are affected the same way."

"Are you crazy? You can't do that!" Bud exploded.

"Why not?"

"Our enemies may be somewhere within range! Or suppose your space suit gets fouled up some way? Anything could happen!"

Tom said calmly, "We can't just sit up here and do nothing. As it is, we're not even sure of our ship's position in space. Anyhow, Bud, I doubt if going outside will put me in any physical danger."

Realizing Tom's mind was made up, Bud de-

cided to accompany the young inventor. The two boys left Bob Jeffers in charge and quickly donned their ponderous space suits and transparent helmets. Then they made their way through the rocket's air lock. Tom took with him a portable sextant and a small portable computer, powered by a solar battery.

Floating free in the space void, Tom used the sextant, then tuned several adjustments on the computer for a bearing on three separate stars. The resulting "fix" showed instantly on the com-

puter's dial—a reading of their orbital position with respect to earth.

"What's the answer?" Bud signaled over his suit radio.

"We're off course for the space station," Tom replied grimly. "Way off, in fact. That means both our ship's instruments *and* steering mechanism were affected." He added thoughtfully, "Our suits seem to be functioning okay, though. Let's see if our jets work all right."

Both boys triggered their suit jets and found themselves able to move freely in any direction at will.

"That proves it," Tom radioed to his pal. "We'll have to—"

Tom broke off as a yell from Bud came over his suit radio. "Watch it, skipper! Meteor coming from one o'clock!"

Tom stepped up his jet power barely in time to dodge the whizzing meteor. It flashed past at blinding speed, almost grazing the hull of the rocket ship!

"Whew!" Tom gasped weakly in relief. "Thanks, Bud, for the warning!" But there was no time to waste. "Bud, you and I will have to locate the space outpost with this sextant and guide the ship there," he radioed.

"Roger!"

Tom radioed orders to the ship's crew to follow the two boys. Then, after estimating the proper course to the sky wheel from the computer reading, Tom and Bud started ahead through the awesome darkness of space.

Inside the cargo rocket, Bob Jeffers switched the automatic pilot to manual control and gunned the steering motors. But the ship failed to respond!

Meanwhile, the space-suited figures of Tom and Bud were already dwindling from view in the darkness far ahead.

"Hold it, skipper!" Bob Jeffers cried over the radio. "Hey! I said, hold it! We can't move out of orbit!"

Receiving no response, Jeffers tried again. "Spaceship to Tom! Spaceship to Tom! . . . Can you read me, skipper?"

Again no response. The two boys were apparently unable to pick up the ship's distress signal!

CHAPTER VI

A HAZARDOUS ROCKET TRIP

NEITHER Tom nor Bud was aware of what had happened to the cargo rocket, which lay marooned far behind them. The two boys pushed steadily forward in their space suits.

"Sure we're headed on the right course?" Bud radioed after a while.

Tom glanced at a small dial on his sleeve. "As nearly as I can figure," he replied. "Our present velocity should carry us up to the space station's orbit. The trick will be to intersect the orbit at the right position. I'll check again, after a time, by shooting another fix."

Ten or fifteen minutes later Tom took the stellar sextant out of its case, swinging from his suit. As he tuned in once more for a set of star bearings, Bud happened to glance behind them. The blood drained from his face.

"Skipper!" Bud exclaimed. "The ship's gone!"

Tom whirled to look himself. The cargo rocket was nowhere in sight!

"Good night!" the young inventor murmured. "I don't see how it could have lost us, Bud. We should have been in direct view from the flight compartment at all times."

"Yes, but remember, the ship's steering mechanism was fouled up!" Bud shot back over his suit radio.

"You're so right, pal," Tom acknowledged ruefully. "We should have checked before to make sure they were able to follow our course. What a couple of goofs we are!"

Tom tuned his suit transmitter for the strongest possible output, then began beaming a call to the lost spaceship.

"Tom to Swift Cargo! . . . Can you read me?"

Bud Barclay joined in trying for a response. But neither astronaut was able to raise the slightest recognition.

"Now what?" Bud asked tersely when they finally gave up.

"Let's get our fix first," Tom rejoined. He finished tuning the star bearings, then read the dial. "Well, we're on the beam. At least that's one thing to be thankful for." He paused, then added, "But we're now approximately halfway between the space station and the point where we left the rocket ship. Do we go back and try to find it, or should we head for help at the outpost?"

The boys' eyes met in a worried gaze through their transparent bubble helmets. Suddenly Bud chuckled. "Guess there's only one solution, pal. How do we flip a coin in space?"

Tom grinned too. "I'm afraid I didn't bring any 'mad' money for a ride back home, fly boy. But I guess we might use a tool from our suit kits."

Tom unzipped a pouch on the right leg of his space suit and pulled out a small lightweight magnesium-vanadium hammer. "Here—catch! 'Heads' we keep going to the outpost."

As Tom tossed the hammer toward his friend, Bud reached out to grab it. But with velocity in space easy to misjudge, the hammer went flying past his outstretched gauntlet!

Tom gave a hoot as his pal started away in pursuit of the flying tool. "Busher! You'll never make the big leagues that way!"

Bud's chortle came back over the radio. "This is what you call *really* going way out in left field for a fly!"

The copilot finally overtook the hammer and managed to snag it by the head. "Outpost it is, pal!" he reported as he zoomed back toward Tom.

Both boys were conscious of an eerie feeling as they trekked through the limitless void of space. Would they be able to reach their hoped-for destination?

Relief surged through them as the outpost in space presently loomed into view dead ahead. This was mankind's first space station on the road to the planets. The majestic silver sky wheel had been designed and engineered by Tom Jr.

Twelve gigantic spokes jutted from its central hub. One of the spokes, serving as an astronomical observatory, bore a huge latticework telescope. Another—Tom's solar-battery "factory"—carried huge mirrors for reflecting sunlight onto the battery-charging production lines. The communication department's spoke bristled with antennas and radar scanners, while in other spokes were the crew's quarters, Tom's private laboratory, and station workshops.

"Station to spacemen! . . . Report, please!"

Tom and Bud answered the challenge by identifying themselves in code to the station's radioman. Moments later, they were admitted through the wheel's air lock.

"Are you two all right?" Ken Horton, the station commander, greeted the boys anxiously as they removed their space helmets.

"We are now," Tom replied with a grin. "But flying up here alone was a big risk."

Ken shook hands with both boys warmly. "Sure gave us a start when our radarman first spotted you. What happened to your spaceship?"

Horton, a slender man of about thirty with dark, close-cropped hair, was an ex-Army major. He had been one of Tom's first space trainees and had helped build the sky wheel.

Tom explained how their cargo rocket had mysteriously strayed off course and later had failed to follow the two boys according to instructions.

"Has it reported by radio?" Tom asked, when he had finished briefing Ken Horton.

Ken shook his head worriedly. "Not yet. In fact we tried to contact you when the rocket failed to arrive on schedule, but we got no response. We checked with Fearing a while ago, but they had had no word either."

Tom mulled over the situation grimly. Had the ship and its crew been kidnaped?

"It may be that our enemy has jammed the ship's transmitter," Tom conjectured. "They could do it easily enough if they're the ones who were able to affect our controls."

"But the jamming would have blitzed our suit radios too," Bud objected.

"Not necessarily," Tom replied. "Remember, our suits functioned perfectly—and I think I know why."

"Why?" Ken asked with a frown.

"Our space suits not only have a Tomasite coating, but they're also insulated with a layer of lead foil," Tom explained. "On the other hand, the cargo rocket has only its hull coated with Tomasite."

Bud snapped his fingers excitedly. "I get it! Those enemy waves couldn't penetrate our suits because of the double protection. But they *could* get through the Tomasite alone!"

Tom nodded. "Right. There must be a special reaction between the lead and the Tomasite—one we have not learned about as yet. Luckily, our C-type cargo rockets have both lead *and* Tomasite insulation. So, if my hunch is correct, our enemy won't be able to foul them up. I think they're our best bet!"

Tom rushed to the communications compartment and radioed orders to Fearing to blast off a C-type ship for the space station as soon as possible.

"Roger," the Fearing operator responded. After a check with the launching area, he added, "They can have one on the pad ready for blast-off in less than two hours."

A tense wait followed. Tom and Bud ate a hot meal and tried to force themselves to nap. When they finally managed to drop off to sleep, it seemed only a few minutes before a crewman was shaking them awake.

"The cargo rocket is here, skipper!" he reported to Tom.

The newly arrived ship, specially designed for shuttle service to the outpost, was clamped to the space station's entry port. Tom and Bud hurried aboard through the air locks, lugging their space suits with them.

First, Tom fed all the data on the missing rocket's last known position into the Spacelane Brain. Then he took the controls and switched on the gyros to pivot the ship to reverse position. He then fired the rocket motors. The braking effect of the blast slowed the cargo rocket and the centrifugal force was reduced. Now the pull of gravity caused the ship to curve earthward in a steep glide.

"Man the telescope, Bud," the young inventor ordered. "I'll watch on radar."

"Aye, aye, skipper!"

Tom took up position behind the ship's radarman and watched the screen intently. Fifteen minutes later twin blips appeared on the scope, faint but close together.

"Two objects dead ahead, Bud!" Tom sang out. "They could be rockets. Can you make them out?"

Bud swung the telescope into position. His face flushed with excitement. "They're rockets all right, skipper. But I can't tell yet whether or not one is ours and the other an enemy!"

Grimly Tom stepped back to the controls, one hand poised to switch the automatic pilot to manual in case an emergency maneuver became necessary. His ship raced onward toward the two unknown rockets!

CHAPTER VII

NIGHT ALARM

A MOMENT later Bud gave a yell. "The starboard rocket is ours, skipper! The other's a type I never saw before."

"Let me look."

Bud slid aside hastily. Tom glanced through the eyepiece, but was unable to identify the mystery ship to port. Was it their enemy preparing to board the stranded Swift cargo ship?

Even as the question flashed through Tom's mind, a shower of sparks burst from the unknown ship's tubes.

"Ion drive!" Tom exclaimed. Like a comet, the ship was already streaking off.

Rather than give chase, Tom felt it more important to see to the safety of the marooned Swift crew. He brought his ship alongside and reversed flight position by gyro. Then he metered a fresh burst on the steering motors to equalize his own

ship's orbital velocity with that of the stranded
rocket.

Tom and Bud hastily donned their space suits
and stepped outside. A brief squirt from their
suit jets carried them to the other rocket's entry
hatch. After passing through the air lock, they
were greeted by a rousing welcome from Bob
Jeffers and the rest of the crew.

"Boy, are we ever glad to see *you!*" Bob exclaimed as the crewmen clustered around the two
boys.

"What happened after we left?" Tom asked.

"Couldn't maneuver the ship out of orbit," Bob
replied. "I tried to signal you over the radio but
got no response."

"No wonder. Your signal never came through,"
Bud put in.

Tom explained his theory that their enemy had
managed to silence the ship's transmitter, probably because the rocket had no lead insulation.
Then he went on, "Bob, what about that mystery
ship we chased away just now?"

"Mystery ship's a good name for it," Jeffers
replied. "We couldn't figure out who it was, or
what it was up to. But I can tell you one thing—
we sure didn't like the looks of it. I have a hunch
that they were just getting set to board us when
you showed up."

Bud whistled. "Narrow squeak."

Tom asked if the ship had ports or a cabin pane.

"I mean, were you able to catch a glimpse of who was manning it?"

Jeffers shook his head. "She had ports, but they were covered. We tried making radio contact, but got no answer—either we weren't getting through or they were keeping mum."

Tom scowled. He realized it was now hopeless to chase the enemy ship, even if there had been any means of overpowering it.

"Let's try the rocket motors again," he said finally.

Switching back to automatic pilot, Tom fed a return flight tape to Fearing Island into the Space-lane Brain. The machine accepted the message and appeared to be purring smoothly into action. But a glance through the cabin's transparent canopy showed that the ship was failing to stir from its position alongside the cargo rocket.

"We're stalled cold," Bud muttered grimly.

"Looks as though we'll have to tow it back to Fearing," Tom decided.

A reel of metal cable, lightweight but immensely strong, was rolled out of the cargo rocket's hatch. Tom and Bud, in their space suits, secured the ends of the cable to special fittings on the two craft. Then Tom returned to the cargo rocket, while Bud was detailed to convoy the disabled ship on the flight back to earth.

Again Tom executed a gyro-reverse and fired his steering rockets to brake orbital velocity. The ship shuddered and peeled from orbit. A split second later came a tremendous jolt as the cable snapped taut, pulling the stranded rocket ship in their wake.

Then came the plunge earthward at dazzling speed; next, the sensation of returning gravity as they bit into the atmosphere. Around the night side of earth the ships whizzed like glowing comets —across the North American continent, and finally into a safe landing on Fearing Island.

Bob Jeffers squeezed Tom's hand after the spaceships' crews had disembarked. "Thanks for getting us home again, skipper," he said simply. Others clustered around to voice the same sentiment.

Tom was touched, and grinned in embarrassment. "Sorry we got stranded, fellows. If I'd known what our enemy had up his sleeve, I wouldn't have led you into such a fix."

Tom and Bud flew back to Enterprises by jet. Right after landing, Tom went to the security department to report to Harlan Ames what had happened in space.

"There's only one good thing I can say about it," Ames remarked. "Your enemy evidently isn't ready to fight with deadly weapons yet. But they may be soon."

Tom agreed. "We're alerted, anyhow."

Taking leave of Ames, he went over to Arv

Hanson's workshop to check on the progress being made on his space kite.

"We've almost finished," Arv reported, shoving back his welder's mask. "The space kite should be ready by quitting time tomorrow—except for installing the gravitex and the cosmic reactor, of course."

The young inventor looked over the gleaming assembly with a feeling of pride. "Nice job, Arv," Tom concluded, clapping Hanson on the shoulder.

"I'll drop over and check with Felix Wong now on the gravitex," he said.

It turned out that Felix had progressed well with work on the gravitex. Satisfied, Tom returned to the big double office which he shared with his father in the Administration Building. The two began to discuss the recent inexplicable events.

"Whoever's responsible is evidently a scientific genius in his own right," Mr. Swift commented gravely.

"Dad, I think it sounds more and more like the work of Li Ching—brilliant but unscrupulous."

Mr. Swift admitted that he had already arrived at the same opinion and added, "He's up to something unique to have stayed in hiding so effectively with so many agencies after him."

Shortly before five o'clock Sandy telephoned

her brother. After talking with her, Tom called Bud Barclay. "How about coming over to dinner tonight, chum? The girls are expecting us."

"Count me in!" Bud said breezily.

The copilot walked into Tom's office a short time later, neatly dressed in a white shirt, bow tie, and sports jacket. The two boys drove with Tom's father to the Swift home.

"Hi, strangers!" said Phyl Newton with a smile as the boys came into the big comfortable living room. Tom grinned with pleasure at sight of his pretty, dark-haired date.

"As usual, they need an engraved invitation to spend an evening with us," Sandy teased. It was a standing joke that Tom and Bud were practically always too busy to take the two girls anywhere.

"Just a pair of squares, that's us," Bud admitted.

Sandy had set the table attractively for the occasion, and dinner was served by glowing candlelight. The main course, Mrs. Swift's mouthwatering fried chicken, was followed by dessert of piping hot mince pie and ice cream.

"Tom, I hope you're not planning a return flight to the space station soon," Bud declared. "I doubt if I could get off the ground again, after all the chow I put away tonight!"

Tom chuckled. "Better starve off a few pounds. I want to get back to the outpost as soon as possible to work on my cosmic reactor."

"I wish you boys would stay home and work on the mystery," Phyl spoke up.

Sandy asked, "Any new clues on the *Sea Charger?*"

Tom shook his head. "Not since that report from the SS *Dragon Queen*. But if the *Charger's* still afloat, I'm confident the pirates can't keep it hidden from sight forever."

Mrs. Swift adroitly guided the conversation back to less serious topics. Presently she said that Phyl had brought along some new records. "Don't the rest of you want to hear them?" she asked.

"Oh, yes," Tom answered.

Sandy put a stack of records on the hi-fi player, and the two couples danced to a succession of hit tunes. Twenty minutes later the music was interrupted by a loud buzzing growl.

"Someone's touched off the alarm system!" Sandy cried excitedly.

The entire grounds surrounding the Swift home were enclosed by an invisible magnetic field. The Swifts and their close friends, to avoid sounding the alarm, wore special wrist watches containing tiny deactivator coils.

As Tom, followed by Sandy, hurried to check on the unexpected visitor—or intruder—there was a loud pounding on the front door. Tom switched on the porch light, then yanked open the door.

"Felix Wong!" he gasped. The young engineer

stumbled inside and almost slumped to the floor.
Tom had to catch his Chinese friend to keep him
from falling.

"Goodness!" Sandy cried out. "What's the matter?"

Felix was panting weakly and unable to speak.
Tom and Bud helped him to a chair as everyone
gathered around anxiously. Presently, after Mrs.
Swift had brought him a glass of water, Felix
found his voice.

"I . . . I've been chased!" he explained. "Th-
the men may still be lurking outside!"

The excited baying of the Swifts' two blood-
hounds, Caesar and Brutus, from their kennels
behind the garden had already alerted Tom's suspicions. Without waiting further, he and Bud
dashed outside. But a quick circuit of the grounds
with the two dogs soon convinced them that Felix
Wong's pursuers had already fled.

When the two boys returned to the house, Felix
began his story. He had been dining that evening
with friends at a Chinese restaurant in Shopton
called Mandarin Gardens. During dinner he had
overheard a group of four Chinese speaking in
hushed tones in Cantonese dialect.

"They mentioned the name 'Tom Quickly' and
a little later 'the Sea Dog,' " Felix continued. "I
was sure they were talking about you, Tom, and
probably referring to the *Sea Charger*."

"Goodness!" Sandy cried out. *"What's the matter?"*

The young inventor nodded intently. "That figures. What happened next?"

"I was afraid those men would hear me if I phoned Mr. Ames, so I decided to get him and bring him back for a look at the four men," Felix went on. "But they must have guessed that I'd overheard them when I excused myself from my friends and left the restaurant."

It was not long before Felix realized that he was being followed by two of the men. The engineer had abruptly changed course, hoping to throw off his pursuers. Instead, a glance over his shoulder told him one of the men had drawn a gun. Felix had then dashed for his life toward the Swift home, which seemed his nearest point of safety.

"I barely made it," the young engineer concluded with a shudder. "Believe me, I hope I never have to run such a race again!"

He gave a description of the four men. Then Tom hurried to the phone to report the incident to Harlan Ames. Less than an hour later, the security chief called back.

"The police have traced the men, skipper, but we're out of luck. The four Chinese were seen on a street corner, boarding a bus. A state trooper's car stopped the bus on the highway. The driver reported that the men got off near the edge of town. The restaurant owner couldn't give any clues. Says the men were strangers to him."

Tom swallowed his disappointment. "Okay, Harlan. Let me know if the police pick up any leads."

Mr. Swift drove Felix home and the young people resumed dancing for a while. But the ominous episode had spoiled the evening's gaiety, and Bud and Phyl soon said good night.

The next morning Tom had hardly reached his office at Enterprises when Felix Wong telephoned him. The young engineer sounded excited.

"Tom, this may or may not be a useful clue," he said, "but I believe that one of those men who followed me was not a Chinese, but only disguised as one."

"Why so?" Tom inquired tensely.

"Because," Felix replied, "after thinking the whole thing over since last night, it seems as if I've known the fellow before—as someone with an American name!"

CHAPTER VIII

SABOTEUR SEARCH

AS TOM gripped the phone tightly, his eyes flashed with interest. If the man *had* been disguised as a Chinese, he might be someone whose face would be recognized around Shopton!

"Think hard, Felix," Tom begged. "Try to recall where you saw this man before."

"That's what I've been trying to do ever since I woke up this morning," Felix replied. "I just can't place him. I'm sure his name will come to me, though, sooner or later."

"Okay. Let's hope it's sooner," Tom said good-humoredly. He was about to hang up when a new thought occurred to him. "Wait a second, Felix!" he added hastily. "Suppose the man is a spy working right here at Enterprises. Think you could spot him?"

"I could try," Felix agreed.

"Good! I'll pick you up in a jiffy and we'll make a tour of the plant," Tom said.

Tom dashed outside to a jeep and sped to Felix Wong's department. A honk of the horn brought the young Chinese-American hurrying out to join him. They began a building-by-building tour of Swift Enterprises.

They visited laboratories, workshops, testing rooms, and aircraft hangars. Even the infirmary and the security department were included in the check. In every section of the plant, Felix silently glanced over the faces of the employees. Male clerks were scanned in the Administration Building. But none brought the hoped-for flare of recognition to Felix Wong's eyes.

"There's still one chance," Tom said. "We'll go over the daily list of absentees and check their photos in the security files."

Again the boys' efforts drew a blank.

"Sorry, Tom," the young engineer apologized. "I was hoping I could spot him."

Tom concealed his disappointment. "Forget it, Felix. It was a long shot, anyhow, and I'm glad we found no traitors here at Enterprises."

After a moment's thought, Tom added, "Here's another suggestion, though. Eat at the Mandarin Gardens as often as you can. You might recall something that will give you a clue to the suspect's identity."

"Good idea," Felix promised. "I'll do it."

Tom went by jeep to his private laboratory and put through a call to Fearing Island. He ordered the base to have a cargo rocket ready for launching at one o'clock. Then he telephoned Bud.

"Feel up to a return flight to the outpost? I'll probably stay there for a couple of days to work on my cosmic reactor."

"Count me in, rocket man," Bud replied. "If those mysterious enemies of yours try any more monkey business, I sure wouldn't want you floating around in space all by your lonesome!"

Tom chuckled. "Thanks, chum. If we get stuck again, maybe we should start a space taxi service! Anyhow, I'll meet you on the airfield at eleven-thirty. We'll blast off from Fearing at one."

"Righto."

Tom made a final telephone call to the Enterprises cafeteria kitchen, asking Chow Winkler to bring a sandwich lunch to his laboratory at eleven o'clock. Tom made it a rule not to eat within at least two hours of blast-off time. Then he set to work on a series of sketches and engineering calculations for his space kite's cosmic reactor.

"Heads up, pardner! Here comes the chuck wagon!" boomed a gravelly Western voice at five minutes to eleven. Chow Winkler, with a white chef's hat perched on his balding head, came in, trundling his cart.

Tom looked up in surprise. "Good night! Is it eleven already?"

"Five minutes to, boss. Brand my pemmican pie, you ought to stop workin' your brain so hard!

All them squiggles an' numbers you been figgerin' out is enough to drive a cow hand loco!"

Tom grinned and laid down his slide rule as the Texan uncovered the lunch dishes. "Mm! Hot roast beef sandwiches and lemon meringue pie! This is more than I bargained for, Chow."

"Eat up, buckaroo. You need nourishment when you use the old head so much!" Chow eased his rotund bulk onto a lab stool across the workbench from Tom. "Buddy boy says you're takin' off for the outpost."

Tom nodded. "I'll be gone for a few days. Have to work on something for my space kite."

"Then take me along, boss," Chow pleaded. "From what I hear, you may be headin' into trouble!"

Tom shot an affectionate glance at the Westerner. Chow had developed a strong and loyal attachment to the young inventor ever since the Swifts had first met him on a scientific trip to the Southwest.

"Okay, pardner," Tom said with a smile. "You're welcome to come along. But you'll have to shake a leg. I'm leaving for Fearing Island as soon as I finish this grub."

"Ya-*hooo!*" Chow, who had never lost his zest for adventure, gave a bronc-buster whoop and sent his chef's hat sailing toward a wall hook. "Me, I'm ready to haul my freight soon as I shuck this hat an' apron."

At eleven-thirty Tom and Chow drove to the airfield, where Bud was already waiting. Minutes later, they were zooming out from the Atlantic coast by jet toward Fearing Island.

The rocket was standing ready on the launching area when they landed. Two other crewmen who had been detailed to accompany them were waiting nearby. One by one the astronauts rode up on the conveyor to the flight compartment.

Chow, who was eager to try space flight again, settled onto his acceleration couch and buckled his safety belt. "Okay, buckaroos! Let 'er ride!"

"Relax, ranger. We still have to wait for the final check, radar report, and countdown," Bud reminded him with a chuckle.

The shock of blast-off flattened the astronauts to their couches. Flesh and skin were drawn back tautly, turning their faces into grinning masks as they lay gripped helplessly by the crushing G pressure. This eased off gradually as Tom's anti-G neutralator took effect.

No one spoke until the timer gun cut loose the final rocket stage. Then, as it drifted down by parachute, to be retrieved by tugs from the base, the travelers swung their couches upright.

"How's it feel to be floating up here again, Chow?" Tom asked. He pressed a button, sliding back the cabin canopy.

Chow peered through the transparent quartz pane. "A beat-up ole galoot like me may not look much like a skylark, but I sure *feel* like one every time I see that lil ole earth so far down below!"

Bud laughed. "You'd look cute with wings, Chow, flying through the wide blue yonder. Wow, what a crazy birdcall you'd make!"

Chow guffawed good-naturedly. "Reminds me. I left my gee-tar at the outpost last time I was there. Seein's as how you don't put much stock in my musical talents, Buddy boy, wait'll you hear a new Western ballad o' mine after we get there. You'll be surprised!"

Bud groaned. "Oh—oh! Don't I know it!"

Before they had blasted off, Tom had ordered that a constant watch for the mystery rocket be kept, by both radar and telescope. But as they zoomed up to the outpost's orbit of 22,300 miles above the earth, no sign of its presence was detected.

"Maybe Li Ching or his friends are not expecting us back this soon," Tom conjectured.

Bud was not so sure. "Don't forget," he pointed out, "if they could foul up our steering system and silence our radio, they can probably black out our radar just as easily."

"All of that happened to us when we were in a rocket coated only with Tomasite," Tom said. "We're in a C-type rocket this time—remember?"

"Could be they've jazzed up their radiation nullifier," Bud argued, "so it'll work through the combination of lead and Tomasite."

"What's this here radiation nullifier you're yappin' about?" Chow broke in.

"It's a gadget our mysterious enemy cooked up for conking out human brain waves," Bud replied with a straight face. "It could even turn us all loco."

The old Texan winked at Tom. "Conkin' out brain waves, eh, Bud? Wal, I reckon that means *you're* in no danger, buckaroo!"

Bud laughed at Chow's comeback. "Guess you got me there, pardner," the copilot drawled with a chuckle.

At three o'clock New York time Chow served a meal of compressed food pellets to the crew. "This gunk's not fit for a self-respectin' chuck-wagon cook to be passin' out," the chef grumbled. "But maybe your stomachs'll take 'em for an I O U till I can rustle up some decent grub at the space station."

Two hours later the gigantic silver outpost loomed through the astronauts' cabin view pane. It appeared to be floating motionless in the inky void, but was actually racing along in orbit at 6,800 miles per hour.

Tom switched from automatic pilot to manual steering so as to nose the rocket into mooring position. As soon as its air lock was lined up with the station's entry port, Tom flicked on the magnetic grapples. But the expected green light failed to flash on his control panel.

"Hold it, skipper," the outpost's radioman signaled. "Something's wrong with the automatic coupling device."

A check-through was hastily made, but failed to reveal the cause of the trouble. Tom backed the ship away slightly, then said, "Take over, Bud."

The young inventor donned his space suit and went out through the air-lock hatch. Chow and the other crewmen aboard saw him jet across to the space station and examine the couplings. Then Tom went into the station through the entry port. Tedious minutes went by.

"What in tarnation's wrong?" Chow wondered uneasily. "Are they sendin' down to earth for a new part?"

The words were hardly out of his mouth when Tom emerged again from the space wheel, accompanied by Ken Horton, also space-suited. Both carried tools. They tinkered with the coupling mechanism.

At last Tom signaled Bud to proceed with the mooring. As he waved the ship forward, Bud fed a slight spurt of power to the steering motors.

"Oh!" Tom cried out.

The rocket ship had closed in so suddenly that his metal-gauntleted right hand was caught in the automatic coupling!

CHAPTER IX

COSMIC STORM

"GREAT snakes! Tom's caught!" Chow's leathery face had gone deathly pale. "Do somethin', Bud! Quick!" he pleaded.

The copilot was horrified. He tried frantically to back off the rocket ship, but the coupling device was evidently jammed.

"I can't move 'er!" Bud gasped. He had already switched off the coupling's electromagnetic power supply. In desperation, he gunned the steering motors again, trying to break loose by sheer force.

"Hold it!" Ken Horton's voice came coolly over the radio. "You'll drag the whole station out of position. I'll have to free Tom manually."

Bud cut the motors, then watched in gnawing fear with the other astronauts as Horton went to work with his tools. If Tom's gauntlet were torn open enough to let air leak from the suit, the pressure would drop and his body might literally explode in the vacuum!

The next few moments seemed endless. Suddenly they saw Tom pull his arm free. His right gauntlet had been severed by the coupling, and he was clutching the sleeve of his space suit with his left hand!

Bud blanched in horror and backed the ship off instantly. To everyone's amazement, they saw Tom—apparently uninjured—dash into the space station's entry port with Ken Horton.

Chow was whimpering, "Oh, I hope and pray Tom's all right."

Bud moored the ship again in frantic haste. This time the magnetic grapples locked perfectly. Then all aboard rushed out through the air lock and into the space wheel, Chow puffing in the rear.

A moment later they were gulping with relief as Tom greeted them with a grin. His right hand was sticking from the cuff of his space-suit sleeve, sound and unharmed.

"Don't worry. Even my fingers still work," Tom told them after they had removed their space helmets. He proved it by wiggling his fingers.

Bud sat down on the deck to recover from the shock. "Tom, can you ever forgive me for pulling such a dumb stunt?" he pleaded in a dry-throated voice.

"It wasn't your fault," Tom reassured his pal. "I gave you the go-ahead signal and I saw the ship coming. But my metal gauntlet got trapped by the magnetic pull of the coupling as soon as it started functioning properly. I couldn't yank it loose in time. I couldn't even talk over my suit radio. Apparently the magnetism set up an induction current that jammed my signal output."

Bud mopped the beads of perspiration from his forehead. Chow and the other two crewmen were still pale.

"I don't see how you escaped losing a hand, skipper," one crewman said.

"As soon as I realized my gauntlet was stuck to the coupling, I pulled my hand up the sleeve," Tom explained. "Just in the nick of time, too. Luckily I was able to seal my sleeve almost airtight by clutching it with my other gauntlet—otherwise I'd *really* have been in a mess!"

"Brand my armadillo soup, I don't never want to see such a close call again!" Chow muttered weakly. "Can't somethin' be done to make sure it don't happen twice?"

"He's right, Tom," said Ken Horton. "I'll post a standing order that from now on no crewman ever works on the magnetic coupling without wearing some kind of nonmagnetic space gauntlets."

Still somewhat shaken by their leader's narrow escape, the visitors relaxed for a time in the lounge of the space station. Chow, meanwhile, had taken over the galley and served Tom's group steaming cups of hot cocoa.

"Boy, this stuff sure restores the circulation, Chow!" Tom said with a grateful grin.

He was just drinking the last mouthful when an alarm bell shrilled in the compartment. An instant later Tom and his friends felt a slight jerk and the space station began to whirl!

"Hang on, everybody!" Tom cried.

The mammoth wheel began to spin faster. Bud and the two crewmen, caught by surprise, were thrown from their seats. Chow hit the deck with a resounding thump. Tom grabbed onto a bulk-head fitting just in time to keep himself erect.

Within seconds, the station was twirling at a dizzy rate. The cocoa mugs had been wrenched from the men's hands, splashing hot liquid in all directions. Fortunately, all other objects in the lounge were securely fastened down against any such emergency.

Bud, Chow, and the two crewmen clung desperately to whatever they could reach—but not before all of them had been painfully banged.

The whirling continued for several minutes. Then Ken Horton's voice came over the intercom loud-speaker:

"Hear this, everybody! The blow is almost over and jet equalizers are being fired from the wheel spokes to counteract the whirling. . . . Repeat: It's almost over! Just hold fast for another few moments."

The twirling had already slowed perceptibly.

Soon it ceased altogether. Tom, Bud, and the others struggled to their feet, then slumped into the nearest seats.

"Jumpin' gophers!" Chow groaned. "That was worse 'n ridin' a locoed bronc!"

"What caused the whirling, skipper?" asked one of the rocket crewmen, who had spent little time at the space station. His previous duty had consisted mostly of cargo shuttle service.

"Cosmic radiation," Tom replied. "It seems to go in waves like the wind."

Tom explained that the space station had no

artificial gravity. A slight magnetic field in the decks was used to grip the metal soleplates attached to all crewmen's shoes. This, plus the slight natural gravity from the earth, was enough to maintain the men's health and enable them to pursue normal activities.

"As you probably know," Tom continued, "cosmic radiation affects all our instruments up here. And a real cosmic storm such as we just passed through can cause some queer effects. In this case, it must have triggered off our station's stabilizing mechanism."

Bud gave a wry chuckle. "I'll bet your solar-battery-charging setup was working overtime during that blast, too!"

Tom nodded thoughtfully. "Another thing, Bud—the danger from cosmic storms is a problem I'll also have to lick with my kite ship, sooner or later."

As station routine returned to normal, Chow headed back to the galley. The larder was well stocked, and by messtime that evening the Texan had prepared a magnificent feast of roast turkey, dressing, and chocolate pudding topped with whipped cream.

"Man, what a dinner!" said Ken Horton appreciatively when the meal was over. "You should visit us up here more often, Chow!"

The rest of the crew agreed heartily. "Maybe we could talk him into staying," one technician suggested.

Chow's leathery face broke into a happy grin. "Nothin' a cook likes better than to feed folks with a good appetite," he said. "I sure appreciate your kind invitation, but I better stick to my reg'lar job—slingin' hash on Tom's expeditions. But I'll treat you to a bit o' after-supper music, Western style!"

After disappearing from the mess compartment for a few minutes, Chow reappeared minus his apron, and wearing one of his favorite loud-colored cowboy shirts. His guitar cord was slung around his neck.

"Already promised Buddy boy some gee-tar music tonight, so I sure can't disappoint him," Chow announced with a wink at his audience. Then, after a few twangs, Chow broke into song in his slightly foghorn voice:

> *"When I left good old Texas*
> *to roam wide and high,*
> *I su-re never figgered*
> *to wind up in the sky!*
> *Oh, my chuck wagon rattled*
> *an' them longhorns could squeal,*
> *But they never went loco*
> *like this old space wheel!*
> *After ridin' a rocket*
> *bustin' broncs'll be fun!*
> *These meteors is more deadly*
> *than a spittin' six-gun!*
> *When I'm through herdin' cows*
> *on the great Milky Way,*
> *I'll head home to Texas*
> *an' that's where I'll stay!"*

The cowpoke's audience was howling with laughter long before he finished. At the final twang of Chow's guitar, they rocked the mess compartment with loud applause.

CHAPTER X

TELEPHONE THREAT

THE next morning found Tom eagerly at work in his outpost laboratory on the development of a cosmic reactor. Most of his slide-rule calculations and working sketches were already done.

"Now to see if my big idea pans out," the young inventor told himself cautiously.

Several hours later Bud found him welding together the outside shell of a huge five-sided assembly.

"Good night! What's that?" Bud asked.

"The housing for my cosmic reactor," Tom explained. "You saw a miniature version of it in the space-kite model. This forms the rear wall of the fuselage, with the gravitex cone sticking out through the center."

"Hmm." Bud scratched his head. "Can you give me the ABC's of how it works? Or is all that too deep for a nongenius like me?"

"Don't be so modest, fly boy!" Tom chuckled. "But, anyhow, I'll try to give you the main idea without getting too technical."

Picking up pencil and paper off the workbench, Tom drew a simplified diagram of what the reactor's final assembly would look like.

"The cosmic rays will enter the screen layer, then pass into the injuster layer, and change velocity in the vacuum layer," Tom began.

At this point, he continued, after the radiation had entered the central part of the machine, flexatrons would absorb the energy of the cosmic rays —thus giving the whole assembly a "push" in the same direction as that in which the rays had first been moving.

"Now notice this smaller housing at one side of the reactor," Tom pointed out.

"What's it for?" Bud inquired.

"That will be the direction converter—narrowing into an output vent," Tom replied. "This gadget will bypass the cosmic radiation, so to speak, whenever we don't want any more 'push' on our kite. Or we can use it for 'draining off' part of the radiation when the input is too great."

"Hey, that's pretty neat, professor," Bud said, slapping his friend on the back. "You make it sound so simple that I get the picture fine and clear!"

Tom laughed. "Good. If it just works the way I explained it, I'll be happy."

As Tom went back to work, Bud mentioned that he had spent the morning in the astronomical observatory, which occupied one whole spoke of the space wheel.

"They're making a study of Venus," Bud reported. "In fact, they let me listen in on some of the signals they were picking up on the radio telescope—but I suppose a space genius like you knows all about such things."

Tom grinned. "All planets emit such radio signals. It gives us a way to check on their heat, since the frequency of the signal depends on the planet's surface temperature."

"How do you like that!" Bud made a wry face. "And here I was hoping to surprise you with my keen technical know-how. Anyhow, I learned that the surface temperature of Venus is a sizzling 585 degrees Fahrenheit—almost three times the boiling point of water."

The outpost's astronomers, Bud went on, had told him that this could mean the planet has a hot core. Or it could be caused by sunshine, since the thick cloud veil around Venus would cause a "greenhouse" heat-trapping effect.

"They figure that means no life could exist on Venus at such a temperature," Bud ended. "It's probably just a mass of barren rocks and desert."

Tom frowned and laid down a file with which he had been smoothing off a welded seam. "Bud, that's one point on which I disagree—I mean, about there being no life on Venus."

"How come?" Bud asked eagerly. "Have you got any space clues which prove there *is?*"

Tom shook his head. "No, my point is that we simply don't know. I admit that no form of life on our planet could exist under such conditions. But remember, earth life grew up from the very first to fit in specifically with conditions here on earth. But that doesn't prove a thing about life on other planets.

"For all we know, entirely different forms of life—forms which we can't even imagine—may have developed to exist under conditions on Venus. Nature is too vast and wonderful for puny creatures like us to say flatly that it *can't do* certain things."

"I see what you mean, Tom."

"Another thing," Tom went on, "how do we define life? As a form of energy? Well, there's energy in the form of vibrations in all things, even inanimate objects such as a stone. So by that definition, there *must* be 'life' on Venus."

"Okay, I'm convinced," Bud said. "I must admit," he added with a grin, "you and your inventions have already made chumps out of too many experts who claimed 'It can't be done!' "

Tom burst out laughing. "That's my pal talking! Let's just hope this space-kite project doesn't make a chump out of yours truly!"

Tom labored over his cosmic reactor for the next two days. When it was finished, he and Bud put on space suits and set up the device on the outside of the outpost's hub. Even a low input of cosmic radiation proved enough to give a small but measurable push to the whole space station.

Both boys were flushed with excitement when they returned inside the station and described the results to Ken Horton.

"It works—definitely," Tom reported.

"You're telling me!" Ken chuckled. "I thought for a while you were going to knock us right out of orbit."

Tom and his fellow astronauts embarked aboard the cargo rocket the following morning and returned to Fearing Island. After transporting his reactor to Enterprises in a cargo jet, he turned it over to Arv Hanson. Both the kite fuselage and the gravitex, Tom learned, had been completed.

"Boy, that's swell news, Arv!" Tom said. "Get this reactor and the gravitex installed as soon as you can, will you? I'm eager to give the kite a tryout."

"I'm pretty eager myself." Arv grinned. "If this baby doesn't fly, I'll be the second most disappointed guy around here!"

Soon after Tom returned to his office, Felix Wong came hurrying in to him. "Just heard you got back, Tom, so I thought I'd better see you right away. I have something to report!"

Tom's eyes lighted up with interest. "About that fellow you thought you remembered from somewhere?"

Felix nodded. "Right. You see, I've been going back to that Chinese restaurant for the past couple of nights, as you suggested. Well, yesterday at my apartment I got a threatening phone call."

The unknown speaker, Felix went on, had warned him in English, "Get out of town or it will be too bad for you!" Then the person had hung up.

"Any idea who he was?" Tom asked.

"I'm sure it was the same man I told you about," Felix said excitedly. "The one who was disguised as a Chinese. I recognized his voice the minute I heard it. He's a fellow I once knew in Hong Kong, named Olin Whaley!"

"This is great news. Go on," Tom urged. He felt that Whaley's Oriental background might be a clue linking him to Li Ching.

"Whaley was a teacher in a school in Hong Kong which I was attending," Felix continued. "One day the police came to arrest him on a smuggling charge, but Whaley had disappeared just in time."

Felix said Whaley was an American about forty-five years old, of medium height, and had a dark complexion. He spoke not only Cantonese but several other Chinese dialects.

"Directly after the phone call," the engineer went on, "I hurried to the restaurant and described Whaley to the owner. I learned that

Whaley was a frequent customer at the Mandarin Gardens, and had posed as a Chinese under the name of Sam Wah."

"You reported all this to Harlan Ames?" Tom asked.

"Yes, and he contacted the police," Felix replied. "A search is on right now, but so far they've found no trace of Whaley. Ames thinks he probably guessed that I recognized his voice, so he disappeared on purpose."

Tom mulled over this information. "You've given us a swell lead anyhow, Felix," he said at last. "I'm sure it'll prove a big help."

"I certainly hope so," the young Chinese-American said.

After Felix Wong had left, Tom telephoned the security department. Harlan Ames had no further report on the search for Whaley.

"But I did have a message from Interpol last night," Ames went on. "The International Police Organization, headquartered in Paris, sent a cable saying that Li Ching had been glimpsed briefly in Marseilles. He had disappeared again, probably by sea or air, before his trail could be picked up.

"And I'm sorry," Ames added, "that there's no new word on the *Sea Charger*."

"Thanks anyway, Harlan," Tom said. "Keep me posted."

By midafternoon, the space-kite assembly had been completed. Tom and Bud hurried over to

Hanson's workshop to inspect it. Everything seemed in order.

"Have it flown to Fearing tonight, Arv," Tom ordered. "We'll give it a shakedown tomorrow morning."

At dawn the next day he and Bud flew to the island base. The space kite was mounted on a small single-rocket stage to carry it up past the atmosphere.

"Wow!" Bud laughed in high spirits as he eyed the fragile craft. "My first ride on a kite!"

Tom's face, however, was serious. They were about to embark on one of the most dangerous experiments he had ever tried!

CHAPTER XI

ADRIFT!

THE boys climbed the gantry supporting the rocket and entered the space kite through the hatch at the top of the reactor housing. Tom sealed the lid tight. Then he and Bud settled into the pilot's and copilot's seats, slipped on headsets, and buckled their safety belts.

"This setup in here is really compact," Bud commented admiringly. "Seems funny not to be strapped to couches, though."

He realized this was because the kite, unlike other spaceships, did not have to attain a high velocity in a short time. Instead, it would be necessary to use rocket power only long enough to reach an area where cosmic radiation began.

Tom nodded. "There's so little room in here we wouldn't have space to lie down, anyhow. But we have everything we need—provided nothing goes wrong."

The control panel stood in front of them, while underneath the tiny deck platform the kite's air-conditioning equipment was stowed. There were also a tool kit, their space suits, and emergency stores.

The transparent dome enclosing the boys had been formed of a special plastic-and-glass composition, light in weight but almost as strong as quartz glass. It was also tinted to protect them from the sun's rays.

One by one, the last-minute electrical, mechanical, and fuel checks were completed.

"All clear!" came the radar report.

"Stand by for countdown!" The voice of Hank Sterling, the Swifts' quiet but hard-fisted chief engineer who was in charge of launching the space kite, came over their headsets.

"... *X minus three* ... *X minus two* ... *X minus one* ..."

Blast-off! The rocket hovered on its pad, then as smoke and flame billowed underneath, it gathered momentum. Suddenly the boys found themselves shooting skyward, gripped motionless by the crushing G pressure of the rocket's thrust.

Up and up the rocket sped, the sky deepening from blue to purplish black before Tom's and Bud's eyes. They were past the stratosphere now, entering the thinning upper reaches of the earth's air blanket. After they entered the ionosphere, an electronic impulse triggered from the launching blockhouse cut loose their rocket stage.

Tom's fingers flew to the control board. He switched on both gravitex and cosmic reactor.

Instantly the boys felt a renewal of the G pressure as the cosmic radiation provided a fresh thrust to the space kite. Almost at the same moment came the countertug of the gravitex, anchoring them safely to earth with a powerfully magnified gravitational attraction.

"She works, Tom! She works!" Bud crowed.

Tom grinned, his eyes never leaving the control dials. For the next few moments his hands were busy flipping switch levers and tuning adjustment knobs to bring the cosmic reactor and the gravitex action into proper balance.

The kite was ascending smoothly now, with a gentle enough acceleration to allow Tom and Bud free use of their limbs. A myriad of stars studded the blackness of the void around them.

"How goes it, skipper?" radioed George Dilling.

"Perfect so far," Tom reported happily.

A series of technical checks with the launching crew followed. Dial readings were being automatically telemetered in the blockhouse, but Tom added to these his own coded remarks about the kite's performance. At last the astronauts settled back to enjoy their kite ride through space.

"Tom, this is really terrific!" Bud exclaimed. "You know, someday people may go space-kite riding for fun, just as they go skiing or skin diving now in their leisure time."

"Could be," Tom agreed with a chuckle.

Both boys watched in fascination as the cosmic altimeter needle climbed steadily. From 5,000 miles above the earth, they zoomed upward to 10,000 miles . . . 25,000 . . . 50,000.

Each thousand miles seemed to click off almost as rapidly as two or three on an automobile mileage gauge. The boys were hurtling through space at incredible speed—yet all the while they were seated in comfort, watching the tremendous spectacle of the starry heavens unreel before their eyes.

"Skipper! Look!" Bud suddenly jerked forward against his seat belt and pointed to the radarscope. A tiny blip had formed on the screen.

Tom was instantly alert. He tuned the radar controls to bring the spot of light into sharper focus. It held the bearing on the radar screen, indicating that the unknown object was heading straight toward them on a collision course!

"Good night! It'll crash into us!" Bud exclaimed in alarm.

For answer, Tom readjusted the cosmic reactor and the gravitex, causing the space kite to veer sharply off course. His eyes watched the scope. Almost instantly the blip veered in response, regaining its collision bearing!

"Seems to be following us," Tom muttered tensely. "Maybe we're attracting it!"

"There it is! I can see it now!" Bud cried.

A flashing object, moving at cometlike speed, was coming straight toward them, growing larger by the moment.

Suddenly there was a blinding glare. The object disappeared.

"It disintegrated!" Tom gasped.

"Or exploded!" Bud wiped the perspiration from his forehead, his face white.

For the first time, both boys realized their hearts were hammering. The whole thing had happened almost too fast for them to be aware of the full extent of their fright.

"Tom, do you suppose that could have been an enemy missile?"

"It's possible," Tom admitted grimly. "Or it *could* have been a meteor."

Bud heaved a gusty sigh of relief. "Whatever it was, chum, I'm sure glad we didn't have to find out the hard way!"

"Ditto!" Tom agreed.

He had decided to venture approximately halfway to the moon's orbit. But as the altimeter needle passed the hundred-thousand-mile mark, the space kite suddenly speeded up terrifically.

"Hey! What's going on?" Bud exclaimed when he found his voice. The unexpected thrust had pinned him to his seat and momentarily shocked the breath from his lungs. "Did you do something to the controls?"

"No, but I'd *better* do something—pronto!" the young inventor replied.

Even as he spoke, there came another tremendous burst of speed, and now the acceleration continued. Tom strained every muscle against the crushing G pressure in a frantic effort to manipulate the controls.

"Another cosmic storm, Bud!" Tom gasped. His words were followed by a cry of dismay as he tuned up the gravitex and conned the instrument dials. "The gravitex won't hold us, Bud! Our acceleration's still positive!"

Their "kite string" had broken loose from earth's pull! The tiny craft was drifting out of control into the outer reaches of space!

Bud could only watch in frozen dismay. Not fully understanding the mechanism of the gravitex or cosmic reactor, he was unable to help cope with the terrifying emergency.

Meanwhile, Tom's sinewy hands were straining at the controls. At length he turned the reactor's direction converter, thus bypassing any fresh thrust from the buffeting cosmic radiation. Almost instantly the G pressure eased as the kite ceased to accelerate.

But even though it was no longer speeding up, the craft was still hurtling away from earth at terrific velocity. Tom sought to counteract this by operating the gravitex at full strength and re-aiming the directional cone.

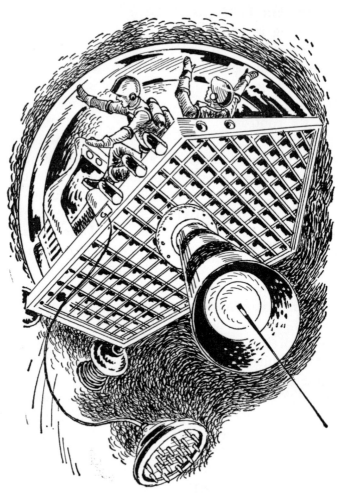

*The space kite, out of control, was drifting
into outer space*

"I'm hoping I can tilt us into stable orbit, Bud," Tom murmured. "That won't get us back to earth, though. Raise Fearing on the radio and tell them to send the *Challenger* up here fast!"

"Roger!"

Glad to be doing something helpful, Bud quickly contacted the rocket base while Tom watched the instrument dials like a hawk. Dilling received the call in the island's communication center and switched immediately to Hank Sterling in the blockhouse.

"I'll have the *Challenger* ready for take-off in half an hour," Hank promised. "In the meantime, radio your position as soon as you settle into orbit."

"Will do!" Bud replied, amazed at how calm his own voice sounded.

Both boys' faces, however, were taut with strain.

"What're our chances, skipper?" Bud whispered.

"Depends on how well I can jockey this crate and how fast they get up here," Tom said grimly.

Bud's eyes met those of the young inventor in another and unspoken question.

Could they survive until rescue arrived?

There was total silence inside the tiny cockpit as Tom bent all efforts toward maneuvering the space kite into orbit.

CHAPTER XII

REPELATRON RESCUE

THE space kite, which had been moving almost straight outward from the earth, gradually began arching into an orbital path. Under Tom's deft nursing of the controls, the gravitex directional force tilted the craft just enough so that it was being tugged toward earth exactly as fast as centrifugal force was hurling it away.

"I think we've made it, Bud," Tom murmured.

The copilot kept a tense silence as Tom's eyes remained glued to the dials. Presently the young inventor sighed in relief. "Okay. You can relax, pal. We've settled into orbit."

"Will we stay put?" Bud asked.

Tom nodded. "Actually, that's the least of our worries right now."

"Meaning what?"

"From now on, it's a race against time, Bud," Tom explained bluntly. "I had things figured pretty tightly for this cruise. You see, our air-conditioning system will keep this coop livable for just so long. Our water supply is limited, too. But that cosmic storm hurled us way off course—thousands of miles farther than I planned."

Tensely Tom added that even after the *Challenger* blasted off from earth, it would take a long time to reach them. "Right now," he explained, "the kite has a high velocity in an orbit around the earth, and the only way the *Challenger* can pick us up, of course, is to have the same velocity in the same orbit."

"Otherwise, one ship will pass the other at too high a speed," Bud remarked. He thought of the hours of waiting that lay ahead. "Maybe we could try hibernating like bears," he quipped. "That would slow down our breathing."

Tom chuckled wryly, then became serious. "Bud, I'm sorry I got you into this fix. I never should have tried such a long shakedown flight in this kite until I was sure all the bugs were out."

Bud punched his pal playfully on the arm. "Think I would've stayed behind? At least we've cracked the long-distance record for kites!"

In spite of his fears, Tom burst out laughing. "Okay, you asked for it!"

The young inventor quickly shot a fix with the stellar sextant. Then he reported their orbital position to Hank Sterling.

Hank's whistle of surprise came over the radio.

"Boy, you really did go sailing off! But hang on, fellows! The *Challenger's* ready to take off!"

The two astronauts settled down to their long wait. To help pass the time they kept up a lively exchange of banter, and even took turns trying to compose comic songs. But the hours dragged by slowly.

In spite of the protective tinting of their transparent dome, the sun's rays were gradually turning the space kite's interior into an oven. Tom watched the temperature climb, degree by degree, on the instrument-panel thermometer.

"How about stepping up the air cooler?" Bud suggested.

"The system's already overloaded," Tom said. "I know it's getting pretty uncomfortable in here, but as long as the temperature is bearable, we'd better put up with it. That'll give us more survival time in the long run."

Tom explained that whenever the air inside the kite was recirculated, a certain amount of oxygen was lost in the process, making the air slightly less breathable each time. Heat, too, could only be dissipated at a certain rate. Trying to cool the air too fast would make the whole cycle less efficient, and thus shorten the "safe" period in which the air would still be breathable.

"I get it," said Bud, mopping the perspiration from his face. "In that case, how about some water?"

Tom hauled out the plastic "squeeze" canteen from under their seats. Each boy squirted himself a mouthful.

"Ugh!" Tom made a face. "It's warm."

"You said it," Bud agreed. "Boy, could I go for an ice-cold bottle of pop right now!"

Suddenly the radio crackled. *"Challenger* to Tom! . . . Can you read me, skipper?" It was the voice of Slim Davis.

"Sure can!" said Tom eagerly, switching on his microphone. "Where are you, Slim?"

There was a moment's pause as Slim checked his instruments. Then he replied, "We've logged a little over sixty thousand miles since take-off. It'll be a while yet before we get there, but we're on our way. How are you two holding out?"

"Okay so far," Tom reported. "But this rig's beginning to feel like a Turkish bath."

"In other words, please hurry it up, pal!" Bud cut in.

"Roger!" Slim replied. He added encouragingly, "Keep your chins up!"

The boys' spirits rose for a while after hearing the friendly voice and knowing that help was on the way. But it was hard to remain cheerful as the temperature inside the kite grew more and more torrid. The carbon-dioxide content of the air was also rising.

Tom anxiously watched the gauges of the air-conditioning system. The boys rationed out the remaining water in small, careful sips. Slim Davis radioed fresh words of encouragement from time to time as the repelatron ship raced closer to their orbit. But both boys knew that a long, agonizing period of waiting must still be endured.

"I think we'd better put on our space suits, Bud," Tom said presently. His voice sounded hoarse.

Merely getting into their suits proved an exhausting struggle in the cramped space. The boys' muscles were numb from long confinement in the tiny cabin, and the slightest movement in the humid heat left them bathed in perspiration.

"Whew! That was worse than wriggling down a chimney," Bud gasped.

After their helmets were on and their suit-conditioning equipment started functioning, the boys felt better for a time. Tom knew the improvement would not last long, however, since the air supply of their suits had already been overheated.

"Good grief! Now my view pane's fogging," Bud muttered after a while.

"Mine, too." Tom plugged his suit radio into the kite's sending-receiving set and made contact again with the *Challenger*.

"We're about half an hour away from your position," Slim reported. "Maybe less—say twenty minutes. So stick with it, fellows! I'm pouring on all the speed I can get!"

Both boys noticed that Slim's signal had come through weakly.

"Our power supply must be conking out," Bud said in a cracking whisper.

"Either that, or the moisture in here is fouling up the set," Tom replied.

The boys ceased talking, hoping to conserve their strength and their air supply in every way possible. Soon both Tom and Bud were breathing in hard, labored gasps.

The *Challenger* signaled them twice again during the next several minutes, but received only a feeble reply. On Slim's third call, there was no response from the space kite.

Aboard the *Challenger* the copilot conjectured, "Maybe their radio failed."

Slim's face was grave. "Let's hope it's no worse than that."

The huge spaceship, with its boxlike cabin suspended in a spherical framework of rails, was hurtling along at blinding speed. Slim gunned the repelatron units in a desperate all-out burst of power.

"There's the kite!" a crewman yelled.

Tom's craft had become visible on the *Challenger's* radarscope. Soon it loomed into view dead ahead. As the rescuing ship drew nearer, the boys' space-suited figures could be seen slumped limply inside.

Slim prayed silently that Tom and Bud were still alive. Guiding the ship smoothly into orbit alongside the kite, he sent two crewmen in space suits out on the *Challenger's* landing platform to attach towlines. The kite was quickly hauled into the hangar compartment.

Slim turned the controls over to his copilot and dashed below. He reached the hangar deck just as Tom and Bud were being lifted out of the fragile capsule.

"Break out two oxygen masks—fast!" Slim ordered.

He helped remove the boys' helmets and apply the masks. Only then did Slim take time to check their pulses. Both boys' were beating perceptibly. Soon the color came back to their cheeks and their breathing became deeper. Moments later, the boys regained consciousness.

"Wh-where am I?" Tom muttered. Then his eyes slowly focused on the man bending over him. "Slim! You made it!"

"We reached you two just in time, I guess," Slim said, heaving a sigh of relief.

"Water! Give me water!" Bud gasped, and canteens were brought.

Tom and Bud sat up, took long draughts of water, and leaned back with grateful sighs. By the time the *Challenger* landed back at Fearing Island, both boys felt rested and completely recovered from their ordeal. Tom phoned his mother at once to assure her that all was well and he would be home soon.

"I'm relieved to hear that," she said happily. "We'll celebrate with some broiled lobster. Bring Bud to dinner."

In spite of the delicious meal and the gay conversation at the table, Tom felt glum. The unfortunate and near-fatal mishap on his space kite's first test still preyed on his mind.

"Oh, stop brooding about your old gravitex," Sandy scolded her brother. "Just be happy you got back to earth safe and sound!"

"Guess you're right, Sis," Tom said wryly. "But I had high hopes for that kite."

Mrs. Swift encouraged Tom to talk about it, then added comfortingly, "At least your invention worked for a hundred thousand miles out in space. Surely that's a marvelous achievement for a first test."

Tom smiled. "When you put it like that, Mother, it doesn't sound so bad. You always have the right slant on my work!"

"What you need, Tom, is a good rest," Sandy advised. She added mischievously, "And maybe a few dates, too—both of you! Something to clear the cobwebs from your brains!"

Mr. Swift grinned. "Sandy may be right, son."

"Okay, I'll think about it," Tom promised.

As soon as Mrs. Swift arose and they all left the table, Tom's first thought was to call Harlan

Ames. But the security chief had nothing new to report.

"Still no clues on the *Sea Charger,* Tom," Ames told him.

On a sudden impulse, Tom made a second telephone call—this time to Felix Wong.

"Hi, Felix!" he said when the young engineer answered. "How about our doing some sleuthing among the people of Chinese descent who live here in Shopton? Perhaps one of them could give us a lead on the man who's been calling himself Sam Wah."

"I've questioned my friends," Felix said, "but none of them know anything about him."

"Suppose we talk to some of the other Chinese in town," Tom suggested.

Felix was eager to go and promised to meet Tom and Bud in fifteen minutes on a street corner in Shopton's small "Chinatown" section.

At the first house they tried, a young Chinese woman came to the door. Tom's question seemed to puzzle her. She mumbled a reply in halting English. Felix Wong then spoke to her in a Chinese dialect. He translated her brief reply:

"So sorry, but I know nothing about the person you speak of."

Felix thanked her and the three boys left. Outside, Tom suggested that he and Bud try another street, while Felix continue alone on this one.

Felix agreed that this might be wise. "If any of

the people you call on speak only Chinese, I will question them later," he promised.

"Good! We'll meet you in a little while at the corner of Ferry and Spruce."

The two boys continued to the next street. It was dingy and dimly lighted, with old-fashioned houses built close to the sidewalk.

Tom and Bud rang the bell at the first house, a grimy red-brick dwelling. A huge, burly American, wearing a jersey, opened the door. His face, revealed by the light of the nearby street lamp, was broad and battered.

"Yeah? Whaddaya want?" the man grunted.

Tom, having expected to see an Oriental, was somewhat taken aback. "We thought a Chinese family lived here," the young inventor explained.

"They do, but they're not home. I just board here with 'em."

The surly giant was about to slam the door in the boys' faces when Bud quickly stuck his foot in the doorway. "We're looking for a fellow named Sam Wah," Bud said. "Do you know him?"

"Naw. Never heard of him."

"Olin Whaley?" Tom inquired.

The question had a startling effect on the tough-looking American. He scowled angrily and glared at Tom and Bud for a moment. Then suddenly his two huge hands shot out. Grabbing each of the youths' arms in a tight grip, he hauled them inside and kicked the door shut with his foot!

CHAPTER XIII

THE EAVESDROPPER

"HEY! Wh-what's the big idea?" Bud gasped as he and Tom, although taken by surprise, fought furiously to free themselves from their assailant's iron grip.

The man's only answer was to give the two boys a tremendous shove. Tom and Bud were roused to fighting rage. Tom managed to hook a foot around one of the brawny's fellow's legs. The next instant, the giant lost his balance and toppled heavily to the floor, carrying both boys with him.

Bud drove a fist into the man's midriff, and Tom followed with a jarring uppercut. The giant's head rocked back and bumped the floorboards.

Punching with his hamlike fists, he lashed at them wildly. But the boys now had the advantage. Their opponent finally gasped for mercy.

"Quit! S-stop it! I know when I'm licked!"

"You'll get worse than this if you try any more

funny stuff!" Bud warned. Doubling his fists, he poised menacingly—ready for instant action. "Okay. You can get up now, you big ape. But one false move and I'll let fly a few uppercuts."

"D-don't worry," the defeated fighter gulped in a quavering voice. "I ain't askin' for another goin'-over. You two guys are tougher'n I figured!"

As the man struggled painfully to his feet, Tom darted a quick glance about the room. It was poorly but neatly furnished with a cheap-looking, red-upholstered sofa and chairs, and a threadbare patch of carpeting. The dim glow of an Oriental brass lamp revealed a bronze Buddha on the mantelpiece and a Chinese calendar tacked to one wall.

"All right, start talking!" Bud snapped.

"My name's Moose Wixman. Who are you guys?"

"Never mind that. What do you do for a living?"

Wixman shrugged. "Stevedore, freight handler, any kind o' job I can get. Ain't workin' right at the moment. I just blew into this burg a couple weeks ago. I move around quite a bit."

"Why did you jump us when we just asked you a simple question?" Bud demanded.

Moose scowled uncomfortably and rubbed his jaw, as if still feeling the effect of Tom's uppercut. "I thought you two were friends of Whaley's. The dirty gyp! If I ever get my hands on that guy, I'll beat him to a pulp!"

"How come?"

" 'Cause he conned me out o' two hundred bucks! Practically all the money I had!"

Moose explained that he had met Whaley at the Shopton railroad freight yards, while looking for work. Whaley had pretended to be a big-shot industrialist with far-flung business interests.

After learning that Moose had just been paid off for a job aboard a tramp steamer, Whaley had offered to double his money for him "in no time" by investing it in stock in a new manufacturing company which he was forming. Instead of doing this, Whaley had promptly skipped town with Wixman's cash.

Tom and Bud exchanged quick glances. Both were thinking, "This fellow certainly looks dumb enough to fall for such a story!"

"Like I said, when you guys asked for Whaley, I figured you're friends of his," Moose said.

"We're only looking for him," Tom said. "We're not friends. Are you sure he left Shopton?"

"If he didn't, he's stayin' well hid," Wixman growled. "I ain't seen hide nor hair o' Whaley since he took my wad."

"Any idea where he might have gone?"

The brawny stevedore shook his head gloomily. "Naw. Just wish I did! I tried askin' around, but I couldn't find out much. Whaley told some guys at the freight yard he was goin' far away—maybe to the moon!"

Moose looked disgusted, but his expression changed to bewilderment when Bud said dryly, "He might have been telling the truth at that!"

The boys departed without offering to explain further, leaving Moose more perplexed than ever. He was still staring after them with his mouth open as Bud shut the door.

Once outside, the copilot chuckled. "I guess that beefeater back there is just a big, simple dope."

Tom nodded. "But that freight-yard lead is worth following up, Bud. What say we check down there right now?"

"Okay."

The boys hurried back to the spot where Bud had parked his red convertible, then drove to the Shopton freight yard, located in a factory and warehouse district.

The yard was closed off from the street by a high wire fence. Floodlights, mounted at intervals on high steel masts, shed a ghostly brilliance over the tracks and freight cars inside. But much of the yard was still shrouded in darkness.

Tom parked near an open gateway and the boys walked through. As they paused to get their bearings, Tom pointed to the switch tower on the hump, off to the right, its windows aglow with light.

"Must be someone on duty over there, Bud. Maybe he can help us."

The moment they started picking their way across the maze of tracks, a bobbing light moved toward them. It was a lantern carried by the yard's night watchman.

"You two lookin' fer somebody?" he called out.

Tom explained why they had come and asked the watchman if he knew anything about a man named Olin Whaley.

"Whaley . . . Olin Whaley . . . Hmm." The elderly yardman shoved back his cap, scratched his head, and pulled thoughtfully on the pipe he was smoking. "Seems like I've heerd that name before, but I don't recollect jest when or where, offhand."

Tom described Whaley from Felix Wong's description. The watchman only shook his head.

"Nope. 'Fraid that don't ring no bells with me. 'Course there's lots of people come around the yard, off and on, 'specially during the day—workmen, loafers, drifters, train crews, hobos. Company brass shows up sometimes, too, and the factory fellers who ship on these lines. Hard to keep track of 'em all."

"How about the tower?" Bud asked. "Anyone up there who might know?"

Again the watchman shook his head. "No one on duty here but me. I jest use the tower at night fer a place to sit down or phone in reports."

After another puff on his pipe, he added, "If I

was you fellers, I'd come back during the day and inquire around. Might talk to the railroad detectives, too. Mebbe they could help you."

The boys were about to thank the watchman and leave when Tom said in an excited whisper, "Hey! I saw someone! Over by that string of boxcars! He was eavesdropping on us!"

Tom darted off in pursuit. Bud and the watchman followed. A second later they saw a man dart from behind a gondola car, then sprint off across the tracks. He was evidently heading for the darkest section of the yard.

Tom and Bud raced after him, the elderly watchman bringing up the rear. A wild chase followed.

"There he goes!" Bud yelled suddenly.

Tom caught a fleeting glimpse of the man, silhouetted for an instant as he dashed across a lighted section of track. But the darkness swallowed him up again almost immediately.

The next moment, Tom's toe caught on a rail and he stumbled to the ground. As he got to his feet, he saw a shadowy figure slip between two boxcars.

"This way, Bud!" Tom cried.

The watchman was now somewhere far behind, as the two boys hastily scrambled over a coupling. But there was no one in sight on the other side of the string of cars.

The boys paused and looked around. A second later Bud clutched Tom's arm and whispered, "He's sneaking *under* the cars!"

Again he and Tom raced in pursuit. A scuffling noise guided them toward their quarry. But the fugitive must have realized that he had been spotted. He crawled out again on the opposite side of the cars, and doubled back the same way he had come. Bud made a tremendous leap over a coupling, and Tom followed.

For the next few moments the boys had the fleeing figure in clear view, dead ahead. Bud closed on

him rapidly. But as his hand reached out for the man's jacket, Bud's foot caught between two rails and he almost went sprawling. Only his grip on the jacket saved him. But the man slipped his arms neatly out of the sleeves and continued his headlong flight.

"Are you hurt, Bud?" Tom panted, running up.

"No! Keep going!" Bud urged, scrambling to his feet.

The momentary delay, however, had given their quarry a fresh lead. He disappeared. After search-

ing for ten minutes more, Tom and Bud gave up and rejoined the bewildered watchman.

"Did ye catch him?" he asked.

"Just his jacket," Bud grumbled.

The boys drove away, taking the jacket with them. They would examine it for clues upon reaching home. Tom picked up Felix who had learned nothing. He was astounded at what his friends had found out. After dropping off Felix at his house, Tom and Bud went on to the Swifts'.

Mrs. Swift and Sandy were watching television. Tom's father had returned to the plant for an after-hours' meeting with a group of project engineers.

"Jeepers!" Sandy exclaimed when she saw the boys' smudged faces and frayed trouser knees. "What have you two been doing?"

"Playing hide-and-seek in a freight yard," Tom said ruefully.

"And ring-around-a-rosy with a giant," Bud added.

Sandy, highly curious, asked about the jacket. Tom spread it out on a chair. The tan gabardine jacket was stained and work-worn, and had a broken zipper.

In one pocket Bud found a small notebook. "Maybe the owner's name is in it," he said hopefully.

Unfortunately the notebook contained merely a list of expenses—meals, gasoline, clothes.

"But look at this, Bud!" Tom exclaimed. He pointed to a notation: "O.W. hooked me for $10."

"O.W.!" Bud's eyes widened. "Hey! That *could* mean Olin Whaley!"

"Right. If it does, Whaley must be hard up for money. Bud, I'd better report this to Harlan Ames."

Mr. Swift came in just as Tom was hanging up. His eyes were aglow with excitement. "Hello, boys," he said. "Big news. Our space friends have just sent us a very interesting message!"

CHAPTER XIV

SOLAR-SYSTEM GIFT

"A MESSAGE from our space friends? What is it, Dad?" Tom asked eagerly.

These space beings had first contacted the Swifts by means of a strange black missile, etched with mathematical symbols, which had landed at Swift Enterprises. The Swifts had translated the symbols and exchanged further messages by radio signals beamed through space.

Bud, too, was excited. "This is the first you've heard from them since they asked your help in curing the disease that struck their planet's animal life, isn't it?"

Tom nodded. "But don't forget those traces of an earth landing by outer-space beings centuries ago that we found in the Mexican jungle. Or that queer-looking wrecked spaceship we discovered near the undersea city of gold."

"Let's hear the new message," Sandy interrupted impatiently.

Mr. Swift smiled, fully sharing their excitement. "The message stated that if Tom and I stand by the space receiver at noon tomorrow, they'll advise us about a gift to be sent to us from outer space."

"A gift! How thrilling!" Sandy burst out. "I wonder what it'll be?"

"Any more to the message, Dad?" Tom asked.

"No, son. I can't imagine what they have in mind. But I signaled back that the message had been received and to go ahead."

Sandy suddenly looked worried. "I just happened to think. Suppose you two can't translate their instructions? For instance, they might use some new symbols you've never seen before. Then we'd miss out on the whole surprise."

Tom grinned. "Not Dad and I."

Mrs. Swift smiled. "I have no doubt that our two space experts will be able to get the gist of any information their space friends may send."

"If the electronic brain can't do it," Tom said, "we'll figure it out as we did when we compiled the space dictionary."

"Let's hope so," Bud joked, "or my old brain might burst from sheer suspense."

The next day at noon, the whole Swift family and Bud gathered in the space communications laboratory at Enterprises. They waited with keen anticipation for the message to come through on the oscilloscope. Even Mr. Swift, always cool and composed, strode back and forth, unable to hide his impatience.

At last the bell on the electronic brain rang, signaling an incoming message. They watched excitedly as the symbols appeared on the fluorescent screen and were photographed, then they quickly turned to the electronic brain as the message was spelled out on tape before their eyes. It began:

WE, YOUR SPACE FRIENDS, HAVE BEEN . . .

A red light flashed above the keyboard and the brain was disconnected.

"Oh, I knew it!" Sandy wailed. "That means the machine can't translate some symbol. Dad! Tom! Do you think you can figure it out?"

Tom quickly pulled the photograph of the symbols from a tray below the oscilloscope. "Quick, Bud! Pencil, paper, and our space dictionary!" he urged.

Bud brought them. Tom and his father studied the symbols as the copilot looked on.

"A mathematical nightmare!" Bud muttered in an undertone. "Just watching those squiggles makes my head ache!"

Not just one, but two symbols of the message proved to be strange, never before received by the Swifts. But Tom and his father got right to work.

Sandy, Bud, and Mrs. Swift watched in anxious silence as the two scientists consulted several abstruse mathematical reference books and worked out what seemed like an endless number of equations. But nothing seemed to yield the slightest clue. Both Tom and his father were baffled.

After minutes of brooding, however, Tom yelled in triumph. "I think I have it! According to Maxwell's theorems, this one is obviously a *field* symbol. And since they're talking about the sun, they must mean 'outside the sun's field'; in other words, 'beyond the solar system'!"

Mr. Swift literally leaped from his chair. He was excited not only by Tom's theory, but by what this implied about the space beings' mastery of space travel.

"Son, you're right!" The elder scientist paced up and down again for a few moments, then seized a pencil and dashed off several more equations which he showed to Tom. "In vector terms," Mr. Swift exclaimed, "this other symbol must then mean a *resultant*—something brought back from their voyage beyond the solar system!"

Tom chuckled. "Right, Dad! A souvenir from outer space!"

The others were bursting with curiosity as Tom finally wrote down the complete message:

WE, YOUR SPACE FRIENDS, HAVE BEEN ON A LONG JOURNEY BEYOND THE SOLAR SYSTEM TO PLACES NOT DISCOVERED BY US BEFORE. WE ARE PRESENTING ONE OF OUR SOUVENIRS TO YOU AT YOUR OUTPOST IN SPACE. IT WILL ARRIVE IN TWENTY HOURS.

"How wonderful!" Sandy hugged her father excitedly. "Dad, may we all go up to the space station to see the present?"

Mr. Swift's face became grave. "Honey, I hate to say no, but it wouldn't be wise to take you."

Sandy tried to hide her disappointment. "I guess you must have a good reason."

"A very good reason, my dear. Since we know nothing about life outside our own planet, any object from outer space *might* be contaminated with foreign organisms. By that, I mean microscopic organisms, invisible to the eye, but possibly deadly to some or all forms of earth life."

Mr. Swift smiled reassuringly as he met his wife's eyes. "Now you mustn't worry, Mary. Tom and I and everyone else at the space station can wear protective clothing. But I think you and Sandy should avoid any unnecessary risk of exposure."

Bud was eager to accompany the Swifts, whatever the risk. Chow Winkler, when he learned of the expected mysterious space gift, begged to be taken along. Since both were veteran astronauts, Mr. Swift agreed.

Twenty hours from noon meant that the object would arrive the following morning at eight. The group therefore decided to take off that very evening for the space station. They embarked by cargo rocket from Fearing Island and arrived at the outpost shortly before midnight.

"What do you suppose the gift will be, skipper?" Bud mused as the boys prepared to roll into their bunks.

Tom shrugged. "Hard to guess. Might be a collection of ore samples from another planetary system. Maybe even a new element, unknown to earth."

"That doesn't sound very exciting."

"Okay. You name it."

"Well," said Bud, grinning, "how about a stardust milk shake from the big dipper? Or a recording of the music of the spheres?"

Tom chuckled and yawned. "You're getting space-happy, fly boy. Go to sleep!"

Tom was up at six, ate a hasty breakfast, and retired to his private laboratory. Chow found him there later, playing with a small, tailless, bowed kite. The windstream provided from an electric fan held it aloft.

"Brand my pork an' beans, what's that?"

"A Malay kite," Tom said. "Very good flyer."

"I mean, how come?"

Tom grinned wryly. "Guess it does look kind of silly, Chow, but I'm trying to stir up some new ideas. Since my space kite didn't work too well, I have to start all over again on the invention. Somewhere along the line I've run afoul of one of nature's principles."

"Wal, you're goin' to run afoul o' that space rocket that's due if you don't shake a leg, buckaroo," Chow warned. "It's almost eight o'clock."

Tom glanced at his wrist watch with a whistle of surprise. "Good thing you reminded me, Chow! Let's go up and take a look!"

The two friends hurried to the observation dome atop the hub of the space wheel. Mr. Swift, Bud, Ken Horton, and everyone else who could squeeze in were conning the heavens eagerly.

"Any sign yet, Bud?" Tom asked.

"Sure! The radarman's already picked it up on his scope," Bud reported. "Your dad says it should be visible to the naked eye soon."

Moments later, a gleaming speck appeared in the far distance.

"Yahoo! Here she comes!" Chow whooped.

Instant by instant, the speck grew in size, and they could see it was rocket-shaped. The missile was evidently traveling at almost incredible speed. As it neared the station, the rocket appeared to be slowing down.

"But not enough," Tom thought with a sudden pang of alarm. "Not even our brilliant space friends can decelerate a missile that fast!"

A quick glance at his father showed that Mr. Swift shared his son's worry. A moment later their fears were confirmed. The missile plowed into the space wheel with a sickening jolt!

CHAPTER XV

THE ROCKET'S SECRET

"TH-thunder an' lightnin'! Are we still in one piece?" Chow sputtered as he grabbed a cluster of pipes to regain his balance.

"Let's hope so!" Tom said. "But that smack probably knocked us out of orbit!"

A quick instrument check showed that the space wheel was not damaged, but had indeed picked up a new velocity component from the impact.

"We're now traveling," said Mr. Swift, "on a slightly canted path from our true orbit."

"Look!" cried Bud. "The souvenir is drifting away from the station!"

Ken Horton rushed to the master-control room and fired carefully calculated jet bursts to bring the outpost back to orbit. Meanwhile, Mr. Swift, Tom, Bud, and two crewmen donned space suits and hurried out through the air lock, taking midget "rocket scooters" with them.

Fortunately the mysterious rocket, made of glistening bluish-green metal, had not yet floated out of easy reach. The five astronauts jetted toward it and nudged the missile slowly but surely toward the space wheel.

"Think it's small enough to go through the entry port, son?" Mr. Swift asked over his suit radio.

"Yes, I'm pretty sure it is, Dad," Tom replied.

His guess proved correct. After the rocket had been maneuvered inside, the astronauts removed their space suits, and Mr. Swift gave orders for everyone to put on protective clothing—hooded white coveralls with gas-mask breathing filters attached.

Tom scrutinized the strange craft, noting its brilliant blue-green luster. "Seems to be made of the same metal as the space ark we received from them some time ago, Dad," he commented.

"Yes, it does, son. Incidentally, you told me the ark had a panel which opened in response to radio waves of a certain frequency. I wonder if this craft opens the same way?"

A close inspection, however, showed that the present missile had a long, ingeniously fitted hatch. Try as they might, the men could not remove it.

Finally Tom said that the hatch probably had been fused in solidly by heat from the trip. "I'll try cooling the hatch to get it out."

He went to the laboratory and brought back a

tank of carbon dioxide. The gas, when released from the pressure of the tank, had a temperature so low that it was able to contract the metal in a matter of seconds.

"The hatch is coming out!" Bud cried a moment later.

"Stand aside!" Mr. Swift advised the onlookers as he and Tom pulled up the hatch from the rest of the fuselage. Everyone gasped.

A strange, scaly reptile lay huddled inside!

It had what resembled wings, folded close to its body. The creature's head seemed large compared to its total size, with long, spiky-toothed jaws. Hooded eyes stared dimly out at the two startled humans.

"Good night!" Tom murmured in awe. "Looks like a pterodactyl from ages back!"

Cautiously the Swifts coaxed and prodded the reptile out of the space craft. It seemed gentle enough and gave no cause for them to fear it. The other crewmen, now over their first shock at seeing the strange creature, clustered around it with intense curiosity.

"So this is the space souvenir your friends were talking about," Bud remarked. "Frankly, I doubt if Sandy would care much for this as a pet."

"Maybe not, but as a scientific specimen it's priceless!" Tom said.

The watchers hastily backed off in alarm as the creature shook itself for a moment and began to open its wings. Then the mysterious reptile quieted again, but its breathing was labored.

"Poor critter looks mighty weak to me," Chow said sympathetically.

"I'm afraid you're right," Mr. Swift agreed. "We'd better get the animal settled somewhere at once and see what we can do for it."

After hasty consideration, the reptile was moved to an empty stowage compartment. Water was offered, but the creature showed no interest. Its torpid eyes had closed almost completely.

The outpost biologists tried desperately to revive it by administering oxygen, force-feeding with a nutrient solution, and injecting a massive shot of adrenalin. Knowing nothing about the creature's make-up or natural background, however, their efforts were useless. The reptile was plainly dying.

"The journey through space, plus being away from its own environment, may have proved too much of a shock," Mr. Swift mused.

"Or the impact of the missile hitting our space station," Tom conjectured.

Working fast, with Bud's help, the Swifts took a number of photographs and motion pictures of the creature. The station biologists also noted down many observations and measurements.

Within two hours, the strange reptile was dead. Mr. Swift ordered it placed in deep freeze until plans could be made with various scientific groups on earth for the most thorough possible examination of its remains.

"Where in the universe do you suppose the space reptile came from, Dad?" Tom asked.

"There may be clues in its biochemical make-up that will help us deduce that," Mr. Swift said hopefully. "Or, if we don't find out, perhaps our space friends will be able to communicate a defi-

*"As a scientific specimen from space, this reptile
is priceless," Tom said*

nite answer to us. I'm sure they thought of the creature as a great gift and did not expect it to die."

The rocket, meanwhile, had been moved to Tom's laboratory. The Swifts went over it eagerly. At first glance the missile seemed to be nothing but a hollow shell. The inner surface, smooth and polished, was apparently made of the same bluish-green metal as the outer hull. Like the animal ark, the present craft seemed completely bare of any machinery or power plant.

"Quite a puzzle," Mr. Swift murmured.

"My guess is that the rocket's built of a radio-sensitive alloy which enables it to be moved by remote control," Tom said. "Same as the space ark."

His father nodded. "Yes, I remember your report. Seems to be the only possible explanation. Well, let's put a sample under the spectrograph and see what we can learn."

The Swift spectrograph, an amazing invention which Tom Sr. and Tom Jr. had worked out together, combined features of both the mass spectroscope and optical types. It could analyze any substance into its chemical components and identify each element or its various isotopes.

Tom began the test by cutting out a small piece of the missile's fuselage. This proved to be twin-walled with a strange mudlike insulation between the two thin layers of metal. The spectrograph showed that the metal itself, as Tom had guessed, was an alloy of several elements—one of them totally unknown to the Swifts!

"Now let's analyze the stuff that's packed in between," Tom said.

Smearing some on a slide, Mr. Swift peered at it through a microscope. The "mud" contained a crystalline grit. It was embedded in a dark sticky binder, which turned out to be a claylike silicate. But the spectrograph showed that the crystals were the same mysterious element that Tom had found in the metal alloy. In crystalline form, however, the metal was radioactive!

"Dad!" Tom cried excitedly. "Maybe we can make this element synthetically in an atomic reactor and use it in our rocket ships!"

"Just what I was thinking, son." Mr. Swift's eyes glowed in anticipation. "What a challenge! Who knows!! If we *can* produce this element, it may revolutionize our ideas on rocket metallurgy!"

"In that case we'll owe a great big debt of gratitude to our space friends," Tom remarked.

It was decided that Mr. Swift would embark on the project at once when they returned to Enterprises, while Tom would continue his own spaceflight experiments based on the kite idea.

Back in Shopton that evening, after their return from the space station, the boys took Sandy and Phyl to dinner at the Shopton Country Club.

Afterward they danced, then went to sit on the terrace under the stars.

"I'm sorry we couldn't see your space 'souvenir' while it was still alive," Phyl said.

"Never mind. We've planned something just as exciting," Sandy said. "A beach party on Lake Carlopa next Monday! And don't you two boys try to wriggle out of it!"

Bud grinned and winked at Tom. "I'll go if the grub's good."

Tom added laughingly, "And if you promise we won't be followed by any spies or suspicious characters."

"Oh!" Sandy snapped her fingers. "That reminds me of a message I forgot to give you, Tom!"

CHAPTER XVI

THE SPANKING *SUNSPOT*

"WHAT was the message, Sis?" Tom asked eagerly as Sandy took a slip of paper from her handbag.

"A man called and said you had stolen his coat!"

"What!" Tom repeated in astonishment.

"He gave me his phone number and wanted you to call him back," Sandy went on. "Here it is."

Tom read the number jotted on the slip of paper, then exchanged glances with Bud. "Must be that man we chased at the freight yard! Girls, will you please excuse me for a few minutes. I'd like to check into this right away!"

Tom went to a telephone in the lobby of the club and dialed the number. A man's voice answered. Tom introduced himself, then asked, "Who is this speaking?"

The person at the other end of the line hemmed

and hawed for a few moments, as if afraid to reveal his identity, but finally said that his name was Alf Turbot.

"I understand you accused me of stealing your coat," Tom went on.

"N-n-now don't get me wrong!" the man stuttered hastily. "I ain't callin' you a thief, understand, but you and your buddy did grab my jacket the other night at the freight yard."

"We grabbed *a* jacket, all right, while trying to catch a prowler," Tom retorted coldly. "If you're the owner and you were doing nothing wrong, why did you run away from us?"

Turbot's voice sounded nervous. "Well, I—I guess I just got scared, that's all."

"Why?"

" 'Cause I thought you guys were detectives," Turbot admitted. "I hadn't broken the law or anything—I just figgered it was smarter not to get mixed up with the cops."

Turbot explained that he had overheard Tom's name when the boys first spoke to the night watchman. The next day when he had realized that "Tom Swift" was not a detective, but the famous young inventor connected with Swift Enterprises, he had decided to ask for his coat.

Tom was wary. "If the jacket really belongs to you, then you must know what was in the pocket."

"Sure. A little notebook," Turbot replied promptly, "for keepin' track o' my money."

"There's an entry in the notebook that says someone 'hooked' you for ten dollars," Tom went on. "Who was that?"

"A welcher named Olin Whaley!" Turbot said in an aggrieved tone. "He borrowed that ten spot from me and never paid me back! Why? Do you know him?"

"No, but I'd like to meet him."

"You and me both, pal!" Turbot grumbled. "I been tryin' to trace the guy for the last week, but it looks like he blew town!"

Turbot's remarks fitted in so well with Moose Wixman's story that Tom felt the man was probably telling the truth. The young inventor agreed to give back the jacket.

"What's your address?" Tom asked. After writing it down, he added, "When can I catch you at home?"

"Well, let's see. I'm goin' out o' town on a truck-drivin' job over the week end. Won't be back till suppertime Monday. But you could leave it with my landlady."

"Okay. I'll do that," Tom promised.

He hung up, then telephoned Harlan Ames and gave him a complete report on the conversation. "Turbot claims to know nothing about Whaley, except that he's seen him around the freight yard," Tom said. "Might be a good idea to check on this guy, though, Harlan."

"I'll do that, Tom, and furthermore, I'll have a

couple of my security boys deliver the jacket, in case Turbot's planning any funny stuff."

"But—" Tom started to argue.

"No need to take any chances," Ames insisted. "I'll find out all about Alf Turbot, and let you know later."

"Swell! Any news, Harlan, about the *Sea Charger* or Li Ching?"

"Not a word. Both have vanished. Too bad."

"I haven't given up hope," Tom replied, then said good-by.

Four o'clock Monday afternoon Sandy and Phyl called for Tom and Bud at Swift Enterprises. Phyl was driving her newly repaired white convertible.

"Boy, how's this for taxi service!" Bud exclaimed as he and Tom hurried out of the gate to join the girls.

"Pretty nice," Tom agreed, and added with a wink at Bud, "Our chauffeurs aren't bad, either!"

"You said it! Remind me to write the taxi company for a formal introduction," Bud quipped.

Sandy and Phyl pretended not to hear, but were enjoying the boys' admiration. Both girls were attractively dressed for the outing in sports clothes that set off their June suntans. They had brought along a huge picnic basket and large tote bags containing towels and swim suits.

"Hmmm, what's for chow?" Bud said, prying into the basket playfully.

"More than you'll find by peeking in there,"

Sandy replied with a giggle as they drove off.

"What does *that* mean?" Tom wondered out loud.

"Never mind, it's a secret," Phyl answered. "And that's not the only one, either!"

At the boys' puzzled expressions, Sandy and Phyl were unable to keep from laughing. But neither would explain their mysterious remarks. Tom and Bud tried teasingly to wangle clues, but failed.

A ten-minute drive brought them to the Shopton Yacht Club on Lake Carlopa. Sandy kept her sleek little sailboat—christened the *Mary Nestor,* Mrs. Swift's maiden name—moored in the club's boat basin.

"Hey! Where're you going?" Tom asked in surprise as the two girls walked right past the *Mary Nestor.*

"You'll see!" Sandy said calmly.

Bursting with curiosity, Tom and Bud followed the girls. They continued past the boat basin to the docks where larger craft were moored. Both boys were astounded when their two guides stopped beside a beautiful thirty-foot ketch.

"Meet the *Sunspot!*" Sandy announced with a proud wave of her hand.

The boys stared, wide-eyed with admiration. From her tall masts to her graceful hull, gleaming with fresh paint and varnish, the ketch was a sailor's dream.

"But whose is it?" Tom asked.

"It's *ours!*" Phyl cried. "That is, it belongs to both our families. It was just delivered Saturday."

"And what's more," Sandy added, "we're all going away on a long cruise in it as soon as Dad and Uncle Ned can leave here for a few weeks!"

Although Mr. Newton was not actually a relative, both Tom and Sandy were accustomed to calling him "Uncle Ned." This was because of his long association with Mr. Swift and the close friendship between the two families.

"What a surprise!" Tom exclaimed. "The *Sunspot's* a beauty!"

He and Bud were eager to examine the graceful craft. After scrambling down from the dock, they helped the girls aboard, then explored the ketch thoroughly from stem to stern.

"A real dreamboat!" Bud gasped, taking in every detail with a practiced seaman's eye. At home in California sailing had always been one of his favorite sports.

Besides a powerful auxiliary engine and a trim little dinghy, the ketch was equipped with every possible accessory, including radio and radar. Its cabin was divided into twin compartments with comfortable bunks and a small galley.

The most amazing touch was twin gravitex machines, mounted one on each side of the hull to stabilize the craft, in place of ballast.

"Dad thought you wouldn't mind if he 'pirated' your invention for sailing purposes," Sandy explained with a giggle. "He had to sneak the blueprints out of your lab one night, because we asked him to keep the boat a surprise."

"A swell application—and one I'd never have thought of," Tom confessed. "I like that name, too—the *Sunspot!* Whose idea was that?"

"Phyl and I worked it out," Sandy replied. "You see, the letters in *Sunspot* stand for the names of all the persons who'll sail on her—at least most of them do. S for Swift, N for Newton, S for Sandy, P for Phyl, and T for Tom. And the U is for you, Bud!" she added laughingly.

"Thanks!" Bud grinned and winked at Tom. "Glad to know I'm a member of the family— I've sure wanted to be!"

"And now," said Phyl, "you two boys draw lots to see who'll be skipper on our trip out to the bathing beach."

Tom and Bud were told to shut their eyes while two strips of paper were stuck between cushions in the cockpit. Bud drew the longer and gave a whoop of glee.

"What an honor!" he cried. "Captain of the *Sunspot* on her maiden voyage! All hands to quarters, me hearties! And look smart now, or I'll clap you in irons!"

Tom chuckled and snapped a brisk salute. "Aye

aye, sir, but please don't sink us!" A moment later he ducked, amid giggles from the girls, as Bud pretended to lash out with a cat-o'-nine-tails.

After checking their running gear and breaking out the sails, the quartet shoved off from the dock. As soon as they were clear of the slip, Bud gave the order to hoist canvas. Mainsail and mizzen billowed aloft majestically. Then, while Bud handled the wheel and Sandy the mainsheet, Tom and Phyl went forward to set the jib.

In scarcely a minute they had left the harbor area and were beating to windward across the lake in a spanking breeze. Bud trimmed the sails carefully, nursing every bit of way he could muster as he gradually got the "feel" of the *Sunspot*. Soon the graceful ketch was spearing through the water at a near-racing clip.

"Nice going, Cap Barclay!" Tom called aft from where he was seated with Phyl. Bud grinned and circled his thumb and forefinger in response.

"What a picture!" Phyl sighed happily, her dark hair streaming in the breeze. "Blue water! White sails! And all this gorgeous sunshine!"

"Not to mention you!" Tom added with an admiring smile.

Turning serious, Phyl asked about the trouble Tom had had with his space kite's gravitex.

The young inventor shrugged. "Couldn't get enough pull out of it to do the job. It was like trying to fly a big box kite in a gale with a single strand of sewing thread." He added gloomily, "I'm afraid it's just not safe enough for extensive space travel."

Half playfully Phyl said, "Well, if your kite spaceship idea won't work, why not make a *sailing* spaceship?"

"You mean, using cosmic ray power to sail it the way this ketch uses wind power?" Tom asked. As Phyl nodded, the young inventor grinned ruefully. "Bud and I went sailing all right in that space kite—downwind and going faster every second! But we just got farther away with no chance to come back. It was like sailing a ship without a keel."

As he finished speaking, Tom lapsed into thoughtful silence. But a moment later he suddenly snapped his fingers and cried out, "A keel! That might be the answer!"

"Answer to what?" Phyl asked, puzzled.

Before Tom could explain, a sudden gust of wind caused the ketch to heel over sharply. Both Phyl and Tom were thrown off balance and went sliding across the deck toward the water!

CHAPTER XVII

A DANGEROUS
RENDEZVOUS

"OH! They're going overboard!" Sandy cried out in dismay. "Phyl! Tom!"

Luckily Tom managed to grab the low rail and hook one foot on a deck cleat just in time to save himself and Phyl.

Bud, meanwhile, was shouting at Sandy to let go the mainsheet as he himself threw the helm hard over. But even before the bow swung into the wind and the sails began to luff, the ketch seemed to right itself almost miraculously.

Both Tom and Phyl were drenched with spray. Sandy had towels ready as they made their way aft and scrambled into the cockpit.

"Good night! What happened to the gravitex stabilizers?" Sandy asked. "We almost capsized!"

"They're working all right. In fact, that's what righted us," Tom replied. "I guess they just didn't synchronize fast enough when that gust hit us."

He examined the gravitex controls for a few moments, then took a screw driver and altered the fine-tuning adjustment of the feedback action.

"That should fix it," he told the others.

"We *hope!*" Bud said wryly. He gave orders to come about.

To everyone's delight, the ketch tacked so smoothly that the deck remained almost perfectly level throughout the maneuver.

"Nice going! I'm convinced!" Bud exclaimed.

"What a boon for ocean travelers!" Phyl added. "With stabilizers like these on a ship, no one aboard would ever get seasick."

"Seriously, that's an idea, Phyl," Tom said. "I think I'll mention them to your dad as a new product for the Swift Construction Company."

"Good idea. And now, please explain what you were talking about just before we nearly went overboard."

Tom said that he had decided to design a spaceship with a keel.

"With a *keel?*" Bud echoed. He looked puzzled. "What good would a keel be to a spaceship? There'd be nothing for it to act on."

Sandy agreed. "That's right, isn't it, Tom? A sailing ship couldn't sail into the wind unless it had a keel to keep the craft from being blown sideways off course. The push of the keel against the water is a force that reacts with the force produced by the wind on the sail to enable the ship to go forward. But in outer space there's no water, and not even air."

Tom nodded. "Right, Sis. But the kind of sailing ship I have in mind won't need air or water. It will use the great flow of cosmic particles in space as its operating medium. Just think," her brother went on, his eyes flashing with enthusiasm, "such a ship will need no fuel or outside power, and will cost very little to build and nothing at all to run!"

The key to his new spaceship, Tom explained, would be a "cosmic keel." It would work in conjunction with the cosmic reactor.

"As the ship intercepts cosmic radiation," Tom went on, "my reactor will convert this radiation into usable force. But instead of just using this force in *one* way, as I did in my space kite, the new ship will use the force in *two different* ways.

"One part of the force will be used to drive the ship, as the wind does a sailboat. The other part will be used as a keel, although of course it won't look anything like the keel on a sailboat."

Whipping out a pencil and a scrap of paper, he hastily sketched a side and front view of his proposed design. It showed an egg-shaped fuselage suspended inside a ringlike frame running completely around the top and bottom of the ship.

"You mean this ring will be the keel?" Bud asked, more puzzled than ever.

"Yes and no," Tom replied. "Actually the keel is an invisible one. But I suppose we'll refer to the ring as the keel. Spaced at intervals all around it will be a number of cosmic-radiation emitters. They'll be like cosmic-ray jets."

"They look like the holes in a circular lawn sprinkler," Bud joked.

"Okay, pal," Tom said. "In flight these radiation emitters will produce an *invisible keel of force.*"

The pilot, he went on, would be able to swivel the ring with its emitters in any direction, on pivoted bearings. Thus he would have a counterforce with which to oppose the cosmic "wind" pressure. Tom explained that this would enable the pilot to "tack" or steer anywhere in space, rather than just drift "downwind" as the space kite had done.

Bud was bug-eyed at the possibilities. "Terrific, professor!" he exclaimed. "A spaceship of limitless range that costs nothing to run! How soon can we take off?"

"Relax. The ship's not even built yet," Tom replied, laughing. "Or named, for that matter. Got any ideas?"

After much banter over very unscientific names, Phyl said, "Give me a little time, professor. I'll think of something."

Meanwhile, the *Sunspot* was plowing gracefully forward through the sparkling blue waters of Lake

Carlopa. The enjoyable cruise drew to an end as the four young people neared the north shore of the lake. The beach where they were to hold their picnic was at the end of a long cove, sheltered by pine-clad hills. Parties of other bathers and picnickers dotted the rocks and dunes.

"Shallow water ahead, Bud!" Sandy warned. "We'll have to anchor here and row through the cove in the dinghy."

The anchor was run out. Then the little rowboat was placed in the water. Everyone climbed in and Bud took the oars.

As they neared the shore, the Swifts and their friends were greeted by whoops and yells. A group of their friends came running down to the water's edge. Among them, looking oddly out of place, was a familiar, bowlegged figure wearing a white chef's cap and a wild-looking sport shirt of flame orange and purple.

"Chow!" Tom yelled and Bud grinned.

"Chow volunteered to be head chef for our beach party," Sandy explained. "And we all planned the surprise."

"Boy, what a swell welcome!" Bud exclaimed.

"It's great!" Tom added.

After the greetings, the entire group went swimming, then played a lively game of softball on the beach. Finally, just before dusk, the hungry picnickers gathered around the glowing embers of

Chow's cook fire as he prepared a feast of sizzling steaks. Appetizers, rolls, salad, ice cream, and Thermos jugs of lemonade were produced from various hampers.

An hour later, Sandy, taking a stroll on the beach, looked out through the cove. Suddenly she cried out in dismay, "Our ketch is gone!"

Everyone looked. The *Sunspot* was nowhere in sight. Had it dragged its anchor? Or had the sailboat been stolen by thieves or pranksters?

Tom and Bud sprang up and raced to the water's edge, followed by the others. The ketch was indeed gone!

Two boys in the party, Pete and Bob, had brought a boat with an outboard motor. It lay beached a short distance away.

"Come on! Take our boat!" Pete offered. "Maybe we can catch up with yours!"

Tom and Bud accepted gratefully. The four boys piled in, gunned the starter, and went roaring out of the cove. As they rounded the point, Bud caught sight of a bare-poled, graceful craft dwindling in the distance.

"I think it's the *Sunspot!*" he cried hopefully.

Pete sent his speedboat racing in pursuit. As they shortened the distance, Bud's guess proved to be correct. The craft was the *Sunspot!* Apparently whoever had taken the ketch was running it on the auxiliary motor.

The speedboat rapidly came closer. Tom cupped his hands and shouted, "Ahoy there! Stop!"

No response. The speedboat leaped ahead, its bow planing out of the water. Within moments, Pete brought it alongside the *Sunspot*. A huge figure at the wheel turned his head fearfully.

"Moose Wixman!" Bud guessed.

Both he and Tom leaped onto the ketch's ladder and scrambled to the deck.

"What's the big idea—stealing our ketch?" Tom demanded furiously. The man was indeed Moose.

The burly ex-stevedore, shifty-eyed under the boys' accusing glares, relinquished the wheel to Bud. "It—it wasn't *my* idea!"

"You mean you're not the only one aboard?" Tom said, shooting a glance at the cabin.

"Naw, I mean it was Whaley's idea," Moose whined. "He hired me to do it!"

"*Whaley!*" Bud said, startled. "Is Olin Whaley back in town?"

"Yeah." Moose said Whaley had shown up in Shopton again and given him his promised shares of stock. He had found out about the picnic and offered Moose a tidy sum of money to steal the

ketch if possible and bring it to a secluded inlet. Whaley would arrive at nine, hoping the scheme had worked.

"Why did he plan this?" Tom asked coldly.

"Search me," Moose said. "I needed money, so I took the job. That's all I know!"

Tom and Bud were inclined to believe him. After a hasty search of the cabin to make sure no one was hiding there, Tom warmed up the ketch's radio and called Enterprises. He reported Wixman's story to the radioman on duty and asked him to contact the police.

"Tell them to be here to arrest Whaley."

After he signed off, Tom asked Pete and Bob to return to the beach party and tell the group what had happened. They promised to do so and sped away. Tom and Bud then proceeded in the ketch toward the spot where Moose was to keep the rendezvous with Whaley.

The willow-fringed inlet lay in deep shadow. There was not a sound except those made by hoot owls and frogs. At quarter to nine Moose and the boys were startled as two frogmen suddenly appeared over the side.

"We're the police officers you asked for," one said. Both showed their identification and said the police boat lay some distance away to avoid detection by Whaley.

After a hasty conference it was decided that the officers and the boys would hide in the ketch's cabin while Moose Wixman remained on deck.

At nine o'clock they heard a faint splash of oars. "I think Whaley's coming now," Moose whispered.

Several tense moments went by. Then the four inside heard a boat bump alongside. Peering out from the cabin entrance, the watchers saw Whaley climb aboard. He was holding what looked like a shoe box under one arm.

"I won't be staying long," he confided to Moose. "Just want to take a look at something on board and leave this package. Then you can take the ketch back where you got it."

Whaley pulled out a wallet and peeled off several bills and handed them to Wixman. "There's your hundred bucks."

Tom suddenly detected a ticking sound. It was coming from the shoe box! He put his lips close to his companions' ears. "A time bomb!"

He leaped from his hiding place, followed by Bud and the two frogmen.

Whaley, taken by surprise, had no time to do more than snarl with rage. Before he could resist, one of the officers snatched the deadly box!

CHAPTER XVIII

THE *COSMIC SAILER*

IN A moment Whaley was handcuffed, and Tom clicked on a powerful flashlight. "Now tell us what's in that box!" one of the frogmen snapped.

Whaley stared wildly at his captors. He opened his mouth but no words came out. Meanwhile, the ticking continued.

"Okay. I'm going to open this right under your nose," the officer continued. "If it's booby-trapped, you'll get the full force of the blast. Now's your last chance to talk."

Still Whaley said nothing. The officer waved the others back, then cautiously removed the cover of the box. Inside was a clockwork mechanism containing a switch which was connected in series to a set of dry cells and a blasting cap fastened to sticks of explosives.

"It's a time bomb," the officer stated. "Set to go off at nine-thirty." He allowed the others a quick glance, then hurled the box far out into the water.

"Whew!" Bud muttered. "Tom, you and I and the girls might have been blown to bits!"

"I might've got blown up myself before I got off!" Moose growled. Turning on Whaley, he exploded with sudden rage. "You sneakin' rat, you didn't care *what* happened to me, did you?"

"Aw, shut up, you double-crosser!" Whaley snarled back, "If you hadn't blabbed to these cops, I never would've walked into this trap!"

The police officers let the two argue for a few moments—thinking Whaley might make some damaging statements. Tom studied the handcuffed prisoner closely. With his slant eyes and dark complexion, Whaley needed little in the way of disguise to pass himself off as a Chinese, as he had done at the Mandarin Gardens restaurant. Realizing he had been caught red-handed, the offender soon broke down and talked freely.

"What were you after on our ketch?" Tom pressed.

"Those two machines your father installed. I saw him take them aboard and figured they must be valuable."

Tom was sure Whaley meant the gravitex stabilizers, but he did not mention the invention by name, since it might give the prisoner information which he had been seeking.

"Did you need a time bomb to steal two machines?" Bud demanded hotly.

"That wasn't meant to hurt anyone!" Whaley insisted shrilly. "I didn't want you to find out I took the machines. By blowing up the boat, the bomb would've destroyed all traces of the robbery."

"And us with it, most likely!" Bud glared at the prisoner.

Tom briefed the two officers on the background of the case. Then he suddenly turned back to Whaley. "Now tell us how you first hooked up with Li Ching!"

"L-L-Li Ching?" Whaley's face paled. "I've never heard of such a guy!"

"Oh no?" Tom's eyes blazed. "I suppose you've never heard of the *Sea Charger,* either?"

Whaley licked his lips nervously and broke into vehement denials. Tom hammered away with questions but could learn nothing more.

Shortly a police patrol launch arrived on the scene. Whaley and Wixman were transferred aboard, both under arrest.

As Tom thanked the two police frogmen, one said, "We'll question the prisoners further at headquarters, and the chief will let you know if we learn anything."

"And it might be a good idea to notify the FBI," Tom suggested. "They may have some questions of their own to ask Whaley."

"We'll do that."

Tom and Bud sailed the *Sunspot* back toward the picnic site. En route, they talked about Whaley's capture.

"He sure seemed scared when you mentioned Li Ching," Bud remarked.

"Yes. I'm sure Whaley is an agent in this country for Li Ching, and knows all about the theft of the *Sea Charger.*"

When the two boys arrived at the cove, their companions, including Sandy and Phyl, were full of questions. Tom and Bud gave a toned-down report of Whaley's capture, making no mention of the bomb, to avoid frightening anyone.

"I'm glad the police have him," Sandy remarked. "Now we won't have to worry."

A short time later the party broke up and Tom sailed the ketch back to Shopton.

Early the following morning Police Chief Slater called Tom at Enterprises. "Whaley still won't admit he knows Li Ching," the chief reported. "But you'll be interested in this development. We learned from Interpol that Li Ching does employ a man named Olin. He's probably Olin Whaley."

"Good clue," Tom said. "Thanks for letting me know."

During the next few days the young inventor plunged into work on the design of his new "sailing" spaceship. He kept at the project for hours without a break, as he always did when fired with enthusiasm for some new scientific idea. Finally he finished the exterior.

While he worked on the interior, Arv Hanson handcrafted a small metal-and-plastic model from Tom's blueprints to show how the new craft would look. Mr. Swift was very favorably impressed.

"I've designed it, Dad, to carry as many as eight persons," Tom explained. "The control cabin will be up front, with another compartment and observation port at the rear, joined by a connecting passageway."

The screen layers, through which cosmic rays were absorbed into the reactor, would be located at the top and on each side of the egg-shaped fuselage. The ring would be mounted upright on a flat, rectangular metal landing deck, with an atomic auxiliary rocket at each of its four corners. These rockets, Tom added, would be used to lift the ship above the earth's atmosphere to an altitude at which cosmic radiation would be strong enough to operate the craft.

"Son, if your invention proves successful, it will not only reduce the cost of space flight, but open a great era of exploration in the universe!"

Tom could not help but feel a thrill of pride. "Then you think I should build the sailing spaceship, Dad?"

"Definitely!"

Tom added, "Any objection if I put on over-time shifts to speed up the project?"

"No indeed, son. Anything which will help our country and mankind to forge ahead in the conquest of space can certainly be classified 'urgent' so far as I'm concerned!"

Tom, who heartily agreed, realized that he was undertaking a great responsibility. He set to work at once converting his cosmic-sailer idea into reality. Round-the-clock shifts, under the direction of Felix Wong, were assigned to the project. Within days, the ship was nearing completion.

Chow walked into Tom's laboratory one afternoon and said hopefully, "I'm goin' along as your space cook, ain't I, boss?"

Tom looked at the hardy Westerner affectionately, recalling how tough and valuable he had proved to be on earlier expeditions. "You sure are, pardner!" Tom grinned. "You're one of my top space hands."

"Shucks! Thanks, Tom." Chow gulped slightly and blushed with pride under his leathery tan. "I already got some good nourishin' grub stewed up and packed in them newfangled toothpaste tubes you designed.

"But how about the drinks, Tom—like milk and cocoa and fruit juices?" Chow went on.

"We'll take those in powder form. The only liquid will be water," Tom said. "We'll take it in these new drinking bags I've had made up."

Tom reached into a locker under his workbench and pulled one out. It was made of elasticized plastic film with a drinking tube attached. "The bag will shrink in size as the liquid is sucked out— that's to eliminate the air problem. I think it'll do away with some of the spilling over and nosefuls we've been getting at Zero-G."

At last the "sailing" space craft was complete. Tom inspected the craft thoroughly and ordered it transported to Fearing Island for its shakedown flight. Early the next morning both the Swift and Newton families flew over from the mainland to watch the take-off.

Phyl, because she had sparked the idea of the cosmic keel, was given the honor of swinging a bottle wrapped in silver foil against the hull and naming the craft.

"I christen thee *Cosmic Sailer!*" she said proudly.

Handshakes and good-luck wishes followed. Then Tom, Bud, Chow, Felix Wong, and four picked crewmen climbed aboard and sealed the ship's air-lock hatch behind them. Moments later, the eight astronauts lay strapped to acceleration couches.

"Begin the countdown!" Hank Sterling radioed.

With a blast of fire, the auxiliary rockets lifted the *Cosmic Sailer* from its pad. Up it shot through the thinning layers of earth's air!

Beyond the atmosphere Tom's hand gripped a lever, throttling the atomic rockets. The G thrust died away as the *Sailer* coasted upward into space. The astronauts swung their couches upright but kept their safety belts buckled.

Six hundred miles above the earth, the ship entered the intense Van Allen radiation belt. In this area the cosmic radiation was now strong enough for Tom to use.

"Here we go, fellows!" he murmured.

His hands moved smoothly over the controls, with an ease gained from hours of simulated flight practice. The *Cosmic Sailer* responded perfectly!

Tom tried steering in all directions, using the keel to counter the cosmic "wind" force. Then he headed outward into space. As the *Sailer* zoomed through the void, all the astronauts were jubilant.

"Brand my biscuits!" Chow cried. "This here's the slickest lil ole space bronc I ever rode, boss!"

Tom was as thrilled as his crew by the ship's performance. But at fifty thousand miles altitude, Bud gave a cry of alarm.

"Skipper! The Spacelane Brain's gone haywire!" He pointed to the skittering needles on the navigational instrument dials.

"The radar sweep's acting cockeyed, too!" called out the man tending the scope.

Tom hastily checked the ship's controls and tried bringing the *Sailer* about. Instead, it veered off at a 20-degree angle. Only part of the keel's radiation emitters were working!

"What's causing that?" Felix asked. "Is the cosmic radiation reduced in this part of space?"

Tom doubted this. In view of the strange behavior of the other electronic devices, he said it seemed more likely that Li Ching and his henchmen were at work. Had he perfected a new and more powerful means of fouling up the Swifts' space craft?

As a check, Tom decided to turn back to earth. After a steep descent of almost twenty thousand miles, the ship's electronic systems began functioning normally again!

Puzzled, Tom gunned the reactor and headed back outward into space. Minutes later, the output of the radiation emitters began fading.

"The instruments are goofed up again!" Bud reported.

Once more, Tom headed downward—seriously worried now as well as disappointed. But at thirty thousand miles altitude, the *Cosmic Sailer* regained its normal flight behavior.

"This has me stumped," Tom confessed. "I can't understand what's—"

His words were interrupted as the radio suddenly crackled. "Outpost to Tom! . . . Mayday! Mayday, skipper! . . . There's trouble here! We need help at once!"

The astronauts were stunned by the unexpected

call for help. Tom flicked on his microphone.

"Tom to Outpost! . . . What's wrong?"

There was no response. Without further delay, Tom sent the *Cosmic Sailer* racing toward the space station!

CHAPTER XIX

IN LI CHING'S CLUTCHES

THE suspense became almost unbearable as the minutes passed. Bud kept trying to contact the outpost, but its radio remained silent.

"What in the name o' prairie rats has happened to 'em, boss?" Chow pleaded.

Tom could only shake his head. "It's a mystery to me, Chow, unless our enemy's killing their radio signal with some kind of wave action."

This thought brought a glimmer of hope to the other astronauts. But Tom remained secretly fearful. Even if his theory were right, it would still not explain the outpost's call for help.

Tensely Tom's group raced onward in the *Cosmic Sailer*. As it drew nearer to the outpost's orbit, the radarman sang out, "We're right on course. I've picked it up on the scope, dead ahead!"

"Give 'em another try on the radio, Bud," Tom directed.

"*Cosmic Sailer* to Outpost! Come in, please!
. . . *Sailer* to Outpost! Can you read me?"

Again no response.

Presently the silver space wheel became visible through the cabin view port. Larger and larger it loomed in the starry blackness.

A radar probe showed no rocket ships in the area, and none was moored at the station's entry port. Tom breathed an inward sigh of relief. At least there was no sign of enemy attack!

"Stand by for mooring," Tom told his crew.

Unlike the regular Swift rockets, the *Sailer* was not designed to fit the coupling device on the entry port. Tom therefore had to maneuver into mooring position as best he could. His hand moved a switch, enclosing the ship in invisible lines of flux which bound it magnetically to the space wheel.

"Okay, men! Into your space suits!" he said.

One by one, they stepped out through the air lock and propelled themselves across the short intervening space to the wheel's entry port. The hatch slid open promptly and they went inside.

Passing through the inner door of the station's air lock, they found Compartment A deserted.

"Brand my gyro, where is everyone?" Chow said.

As if in answer, the door leading into the next compartment suddenly opened. A shaven-headed Oriental, clad in a black military uniform, en-

tered. Several other Asiatics followed, all clutching automatic pistols.

"Greetings, gentlemen," said their leader
suavely. He added with a mirthless chuckle, "Perhaps I can answer your questions. The station
crew are already prisoners. It was one of my own
men who sent you that call for help!"

Tom and his companions were stunned.

"Who are you?" Tom asked icily.

"Suffice it to say that we are now the possessors
of your famous outpost in space."

"Oh yes?" Bud blurted out angrily. "Well, you
won't be for very long! As soon as Fearing Island
realizes the wheel isn't sending the proper check
signals, there'll be American spacemen swarming
all over this place!"

"They'll have you sneakin' hoss thieves roped
and hawg-tied so fast it'll make your heads spin!"
Chow added threateningly.

The Oriental's lips curled. "So sorry to disappoint you, gentlemen. Your rocket base will not
learn of the space wheel's capture. You see, I have
already forced the station crew to return to their
regular communication posts. And each man
knows he will die a very unpleasant death if he
attempts to betray our presence!"

Tom and the other astronauts were chilled by
their captor's ruthless tone. Felix Wong pleaded
with him in Cantonese, but it was of no avail.

Finally Tom said in a cold, level voice, "All

right, you have the upper hand at the moment. What do you intend to do?"

The shaven-headed man gave a toothy smile of triumph. "Ah! You are ready to face the situation sensibly, then? That is most wise!"

Turning to his men, the leader issued orders in an Oriental tongue. Rope was brought and the astronauts' hands were tied, except Tom's. Bud, Chow, Felix, and the four crewmen were herded off to join the other prisoners. From glimpses caught through the open doorway of the compartment, Tom saw that there were at least a dozen enemy raiders in the group.

At last Tom was left alone with the leader and three of his men.

"You are wondering, perhaps, why you were not tied up with the others," the Oriental said. "That, my friend, is because you will be allowed to leave here. We came to the outpost in a rocket ship. It departed at once in order not to arouse your suspicions. We shall return to earth in your *Cosmic Sailer* with yourself at the controls."

"What makes you think I'll agree to that?" Tom snapped.

"Would you rather die at once?" The man sneered. "Three times we have tried and failed to kill you, Tom Swift—once in a car accident, once on a rocket flight, and once by a bomb placed aboard your yacht by that stupid Olin Whaley. I assure you we shall not fail next time!"

"Why are you so eager to kill me?" Tom asked coolly.

The man's eyes narrowed. "You and your father are successful scientists," he snarled. "Your work is prized by your own government. For our chief, that is reason enough to kill you!"

The answer confirmed Tom's hunch about who the scoundrel was that headed the group. "I see," he said. "And your chief is Li Ching."

Tom saw his captors exchange glances of surprise, but no one spoke.

"Don't worry about talking," Tom went on needlingly. "We know all about Li Ching's activities—including the fact that he stole the *Sea Charger!*"

Tom's words caused a stir of alarm among the Orientals. They started to chatter among themselves until their leader silenced them.

"Enough, Tom Swift!" he barked. "We shall leave here at once in your new spaceship!" To back up his words, the man jammed the muzzle of his gun into Tom's midriff.

At least half of the raiders were left behind to guard the outpost. The others embarked in the *Cosmic Sailer* with Tom, who was given a definite course for the return flight to earth. The leader sat beside him in the copilot's seat. He watched the navigational instrument dials intently to detect any attempted deviation.

As they plunged into earth's atmosphere, Tom

As the Cosmic Sailer *broke through the clouds,*
Tom spotted the stolen ship

gunned the atomic rockets to slow their descent. The *Sailer* arced at dizzying speed above the North American continent, then out over the Atlantic. Tom braked still harder as they entered a vast cloud layer. The Oriental leader tuned the radio to a certain frequency and hissed several words into the microphone. Seconds later, they broke through the cloud barrier and Tom gasped.

"My *Sea Charger!*"

The stolen ship lay at anchor in the waters below, berthed near the rocky islet which Tom, Bud, and Felix had flown to investigate!

Its launching pad, cabled to the stern, floated at a distance.

"It wasn't sunk, thank goodness!" Tom thought.

Obeying orders, he landed on the pad and was taken aboard the *Sea Charger*. Two Orientals, grinning maliciously, greeted him as he stepped on deck. One was a suave, slender man with beady, calculating eyes. From pictures Tom had seen, he recognized the man as Li Ching.

"And this," Li Ching said, after identifying himself, "is my honored friend, Captain Yao."

Yao, a stocky man of about fifty, was wearing the same black uniform as the other raiders, but it had naval stripes. "Captain of the great scientific research ship, known by you as the *Sea Charger*," he added with a gloating chuckle.

"*My* ship, you mean!" Tom burst out angrily. "Yours only by an act of piracy!"

Li Ching's lips curled with amusement, but his eyes remained deadly. "Let us say, rather, taken over by the patriotic revolutionary group of which I am chief. We hope that you, Tom Swift, will be wise enough to co-operate with us."

"How?" Tom shot back.

Li Ching waved his hand. "Your part will be simple. You have only to tell us the details of your latest space research, and other inventions by you and your father, such as your repelatron device. In return, you will be allowed to work for our honored cause—at excellent pay!"

Tom did not even try to disguise his look of utter disgust. "And be a traitor to my own country? Don't make me laugh! You're not even as intelligent as I thought, Li Ching!"

The Oriental's face froze into a mask of cold rage. He merely shrugged and glanced at Captain Yao, who barked out a command. Two men grabbed Tom's arms and took him below deck to one of the crew's bunk compartments. Li Ching and Captain Yao followed.

"We will give you twelve hours to come to your senses," Li Ching warned. "Work for us and your life will be spared. Otherwise, your entire family is doomed!"

CHAPTER XX

A DARING PLAN

LI CHING'S threat sent a shock of fear through Tom. Once locked in the compartment, a prisoner of the Orientals, he would have no chance to warn his family of their terrible danger! Desperately Tom stalled for time.

"You're still a fool, Li Ching," he said, trying to sound unperturbed. "Without my help, you have no hope of gaining power anywhere. Since you had to steal the *Sea Charger* and capture my new spaceship, it's obvious you have no scientific know-how of your own."

Li Ching was stung to anger by Tom's remark. "Ah! You think not? What about the way we disabled your space craft with our jamming-wave generator? Or the way we camouflaged this ship from view with a synthetic cloud cover and the illusion of an iceberg? You call that nothing?"

"Waste no more words on the young fool, Excellency!" Captain Yao snarled. "Let us leave him here to choose between life and death!"

Again their faces became masklike and the Orientals withdrew from the compartment. A second later Tom heard the key turn in the lock and Li Ching saying, "If you tamper with the lock, Swift, you will set off the escape alarm which I am now switching on."

The young inventor was not willing to accept his imprisonment. "I must find some means of escape!" he said to himself.

A remark once made by his father flashed through Tom's mind: *A true scientist will always find a way to work with whatever tools come to hand.*

"Good old Dad!" Tom thought.

His eyes roved about the small compartment. The porthole was open, but Tom realized regretfully that it was not large enough for him to squeeze through. A chill breeze was blowing in. Tom shivered.

"Instead of closing the porthole and shutting out the fresh sea air," Tom thought, "I'll turn up the heat a bit."

The next instant an idea flashed through his mind. The *Sea Charger* was atomic-powered and all compartments were radiant-heated in cold weather by nickle-chrome elements running through the bulkhead, close to the deck.

"A high-amp current! Just what I need!" But it would be wiser to wait until darkness, Tom decided, before putting his plan into execution.

Some time later, one of the crew brought him supper on a tray. Tom had stretched out on a bunk at the first sound of the key in the lock.

"You eat now," the man encouraged.

"Just put it down," Tom muttered listlessly.

The man shrugged and went out, locking the door behind him. An hour later daylight faded. Night fell over the sea.

Tom switched on a small reading lamp and set to work. With one of the tools from his small, pocket-size tool kit, he removed the heat-control switch from the bulkhead, so as to expose the wiring behind it.

Fortunately, there was enough slack in the heavy-gauge wires which carried the heating current. Tom loosened the connectors from the heating elements, then pulled the wires as far as possible out of their conduit. They were long enough to reach the door.

"I don't dare touch the lock," Tom said to himself. "I'll have to tackle the hinges."

He held one of the wires on each side of the door's lower brass hinge. Sizzling and sputtering, the current flowed through the hinge. Within minutes, the brass had softened enough from the heat for Tom to pry the hinge apart. He repeated the operation on the top hinge.

"Whew!" Tom let out a sigh of tension and switched off the current. "Now for the risky part!"

He inserted the screw-driver blade between door and frame and pried the door open enough to slip out. A glance down the corridor in both directions showed no one in sight.

Tom hesitated a moment, mapping his next move. Having designed the ship with his father, he knew every foot of the *Sea Charger's* layout below decks. But could he disable the ship enough to prevent an enemy getaway, and still have time to escape himself before being detected?

"I'll have to chance it!" Tom determined.

Darting along the corridor, he came to a companionway and slipped stealthily down the steps. A moment later he was in the ship's electrical-control room. Working by his small but powerful pocket flashlight, Tom pulled out nonconducting tools from a storage locker. With them, he disconnected the main power line at the circuit breaker and clamped the two cable ends together. Turning on the power caused a dull roar from the generator. It was followed by a flash, and smoke filled the room.

"That takes care of the generator," Tom told himself, knowing that the short circuit must have burned out the windings. "I hope no one heard that roar."

He stood stock-still, wiping away perspiration that had burst out on his forehead. When there was no sign of detection, Tom cautiously emerged from the compartment and headed for the main deck. Now he heard angry shouts and the sound of trampling feet. Evidently the sudden power failure had thrown the ship into utter confusion.

"This may help me!" Tom thought excitedly.

Topside all was in darkness. Tom could dimly make out several figures on the bridge, shouting and gesticulating, while two or three others were groping about on the fo'c'sle.

"Now for a break!" Tom decided.

He darted to the stern and scrambled over the rail. Hand over hand, he swung himself along the cable to the launching pad. The *Cosmic Sailer* was unguarded!

"What luck!" Tom thought as he climbed aboard.

Gunning the take-off rockets, he shot skyward in the craft. Below Tom glimpsed the sudden flash of a lantern and running figures on the *Sea Charger's* deck.

"So long, my enemies. I'll see you later!"

To reach Fearing, it would be necessary to rocket above the atmosphere, then make the usual glide descent back to the base. Tom chafed as he thought of the precious time it would take. Could he risk a radio call to Fearing Island or Enterprises?

"Too dangerous," Tom figured.

If the message were picked up by the raiders at the outpost, his friends there might suffer.

It was close to midnight when Tom finally landed at Fearing. He quickly poured out his story to Hank Sterling, then phoned Harlan Ames, who said he would get in touch with government officials in Washington at once and with Interpol to capture the pirates.

"I'll lead a group from here up to the outpost," Tom said, signing off.

The base bristled with frenzied activity as rockets were prepared for launching. Half an hour later, Tom took off again. He used the *Cosmic Sailer,* sure he could fool the Orientals holding the space station into thinking the craft was still in their possession. Then, after landing and taking command by ruse, he would be reinforced with the ships following him.

"I sure hope the plan works," said Hank grimly.

The men's tense feelings grew almost unbearable as the *Sailer* approached the space wheel. Tom knew that a single false move could cost the lives of himself and every man aboard. He had already ordered his crew to don space suits and keep their gauntleted hands in front of their faces in case they were observed through telescopes or the station's view ports.

"They must be made to believe we're Li Ching's men," Tom said.

After mooring, he led the way as they jetted across to the wheel's entry port. They passed through the air lock, then stared in delighted stupefaction.

"Skipper!". . . "Hank!". . . "Yippee!"

"Bud! . . . Chow! . . . For Pete's sake, what happened?" Tom gasped after pulling off his space helmet. "How'd you get free?"

The explanation came out in a babble of excited voices. Chow had inveigled their captors into letting him cook the next meal. Being hungry, and thinking one man could do no harm, they had agreed. But Chow had slipped a knife inside one of the bowls of rice brought to the prisoners by their guard. Bud had found the instrument.

"That rat was laughing out of the other side of his mouth after we cut ourselves free!" Bud stated with gleeful satisfaction. "The next time he stepped into the compartment, we jumped and disarmed him before he could make a sound to warn the others."

Bud's group had then darted about the station, overcoming the other raiders, one by one. They had just finished releasing Ken Horton and the regular station crewmen when they had seen the *Cosmic Sailer* arriving.

"Brand my space biscuits," said Chow, "we figgered we had another lil ole scrap on our hands when you fellows showed up. Sure was a good feelin' to get a close look at your faces!"

"Don't think we didn't feel good when we saw you men!" Tom replied, laughing. "You're a pretty sly old coyote, Chow! And the rest of you ought to get medals, too."

Tom quickly described his own escape, then radioed Enterprises and Fearing the whole story. It was too late to turn back all the rescue rockets. Upon their arrival some were detailed to transport the prisoners to Fearing.

Home once more, Tom and Bud learned the fate of Li Ching, Captain Yao, and other members of their rebel group. All had been captured by American and Canadian naval forces while trying to get away from the *Sea Charger*. The generator had been put into working order and the ship was on its way home.

"The gang's headquarters was in Hong Kong," Ames concluded. "The British police are now taking care of things at that end—and a Navy task force is being dispatched to clean out Li Ching's secret rocket base on a Pacific Island."

To celebrate the victorious outcome, Sandy begged Tom and Bud to take her and Phyl up for a cruise in the *Cosmic Sailer*. Both girls were thrilled as they soared above the earth.

"Tom, this is wonderful!" Phyl exulted. "It's —well, it's out of this world!"

Tom chuckled, happy that he had achieved his goal of economic space travel and space-flight training. Another invention was already taking shape in his mind. He was eager to get to work on it!

But now he turned to Phyl. "I guess a sightsee-ing cruise is the least I can do, since you put that idea of a cosmic keel into my head!"

At one hundred thousand miles altitude, with the *Sailer* racing smoothly, Bud chortled, "Let's keep right on going to the next solar system!"